AF469741

*NOW NEWMAN WAS OLD*

*Other books by Chaim Bermant*

Troubled Eden
The Cousinhood
Point of Arrival
The Walled Garden
Coming Home
The Jews


*Novels*

Jericho Sleep Alone
Ben Preserve Us
Berl Make Tea
Diary of an Old Man
Swinging in the Rain
Here Endeth the Lesson
Now Dowager
Roses are Blooming in Picardy
The Last Supper
The Second Mrs Whitberg
The Squire of Bor Shachor

# *NOW NEWMAN WAS OLD*

a novel

by

## Chaim Bermant

London
GEORGE ALLEN & UNWIN
Boston          Sydney

First published in 1978



GEORGE ALLEN & UNWIN LTD.
40 Museum Street, London WC1A 1LU



British Library Cataloguing in Publication Data

Bermant, Chaim
  Now Newman was old.
  I. Title
  823′.9′1F    PR6052.E63N/    78-40168


ISBN 0-04-823145-2

Typeset in 11 on 12 point Baskerville by
Red Lion Setters, Holborn, London
and printed in Great Britain by
Biddles Ltd, Guildford, Surrey

The author wishes to acknowledge assistance from
the Arts Council of Great Britain

**PART I**

*A New Life*

# 1

'That's it then,' I said when the removal van pulled up.

'You got regrets?' asked Dora.

'Sure I've got regrets.'

'Habit's everything with you,' she said. 'You'd have regrets leaving hell.'

'Sure I'd have regrets. You got no regrets at all?'

'No I haven't. The stairs is killing me. I can't wait to have everything on one floor.'

'We could have let the top floor.'

'*Let* the top floor? I should keep lodgers at my age?'

'What's age got to do with it? And besides they wouldn't be lodgers, they'd be tenants.'

'They'd have been coming through our hallway and up the stairs there, right?'

'Right.'

'They'd be lodgers.'

We had been through all that before, if not a hundred times then a thousand times, and of course she was right. The house was big, it was difficult to get help (and expensive when you could get it), and the stairs were awkward.

'It's all right for you,' she used to say. 'When you come downstairs in the mornings that's you downstairs till you go to bed at night, but me I'm up and down, down and up a hundred times a day.'

She was house-proud. I also liked a tidy room, but if the door was closed and I couldn't see inside, it didn't worry me if it was covered in dust, but not Dora, bless her. She'd go on a tour of inspection, and if a speck of dust had landed some-where she'd be upon it with a little whoop of glee. And it wasn't only the rooms. If there was a suit in the house which I wasn't wearing, it was in the dry cleaners. She sent curtains to the dry cleaners, carpets to the dry cleaners, and where

the carpets were fitted, the dry cleaners came to us. She was
God's gift to the cleaning trade. 'A house is to live in,' said
one of the children, 'it's not Marks and Spencer', but you
couldn't argue with Dora, or at least you could, but it
wouldn't get you anywhere and so of course when I retired
from business we decided to move. *We* decided? She
decided, and as a matter of fact it was she who decided that
I should retire from business in the first place.

I had built up a nice little company importing Scandinavian
knitwear, which had its ups and downs but on the whole the
ups were better than the downs and I was not doing too
badly. There were people in the same line of business who
offered to take me over and of course I ignored them, first
because their offers didn't amount to much and second of
all because I liked the business. What would I do with
myself if I sold out?

One day I was discussing yet another offer when Dora
happened to come into the office.

'Don't mind me if I listen,' she said, 'I'm also a partner.'

As a matter of fact I did mind because although she was
technically a director of the company I didn't like her inter-
fering in the business and as a rule she didn't, but when I got
home in the evening she said:

'Well, did you sell?'

'Of course not.'

'Why not?'

'He didn't offer nearly enough.'

'Did you ask for more?'

'No.'

'Why not?'

'Because I'm not interested in selling.'

'*I'm* interested in selling. Ask for more.'

I didn't argue with her but asked for a ridiculous price
which I was sure would be rejected out of hand, but he
made another offer and then another and came so near to
the figure I asked that I would have been crazy to refuse, but
when I accepted I thought I must have been crazy to listen

to him or to my wife. There's more to being in business than
money. It was a way of life. I was only sixty-six and, except
for a bronchial disorder here and a stomach complaint
there, fit and in the prime of life. Dora was a year older
(three years older I suspect, but it wasn't a matter she liked
to discuss), but she would always find things to send to the
dry cleaner and dust to hunt down, and food to cook and
beds to make and presents to make up for this grandchild's
birthday or that daughter's wedding anniversary, but what
would I do with myself?

It was a question which I had asked only once before in
my life. I had built up the business with the help of my
brother David—some would say in spite of his help, for he
wasn't much of a businessman—but we were very close. I
always tried out ideas on him and if he sounded enthusias-
tic, it was a good enough reason to turn them down. We
would argue, of course, with Iris, my secretary (I call her
secretary, but she was almost the boss), pitching in on his
side or mine. Anyone passing our office would think someone was being killed, for we (or at least David and I) thought
at the tops of our voices, but that was how we settled our
affairs and on the whole it worked.

Then David died. He was younger than me, hardly more
than forty, and for a while I couldn't face the office. We had
formed a sort of family—he, Iris and I—a querulous family,
perhaps, but a close one, and we depended a lot on each
other. Now Dave was gone, everything else seemed to fall
away. I wanted to sell the business, give it away, and if Iris
hadn't been around to look after things (you always need a
goy in a firm to keep his head when everybody else is losing
theirs), it might have folded on its own accord. But then I
gradually came to my senses. I still found it difficult to take
up the old routine, but if I didn't go back to the business,
what else could I do with myself?

The day I left my office was one of the saddest in my life.
Even Iris kept wiping her eyes and complaining that she was
having another bout of hay fever. I was in tears myself. I

had thirty-two people working for me. Some of them had been with me from the time I started after the war. I had been like a father to them, lent them money to set up home, attended their weddings, their christenings, Barmitzvahs, helped their children get jobs. If they were sick I'd visit them in hospital, or Dora would (which didn't always speed their recovery). If they went on holiday they'd send me picture postcards (Dora sometimes complained, 'If your workers can afford to go to the Canaries, how come you grumble when I want a weekend in Bournemouth?'). My voice broke several times at the farewell dinner, but by way of irony they presented me with a silver gardening fork, with the inscription 'with best wishes for a long and happy retirement'.

That, I suppose, is what every Englishman thinks of when he thinks of retirement: planting herbaceous borders here, rambling roses there, clipping hedges, mowing lawns, watering geraniums. English I am, but that English I'm not. People speak of green fingers and even goldfinger, well I'm black fingers: everything I touch wilts. Still I didn't mind pottering about in the garden on a Sunday morning, but when it came to the fancy stuff—and Dora liked the garden to look as tidy as the drawing room—we got a gardener.

Two people gave me private gifts. One was Leslie, our storeman, the oldest member of the firm, a bachelor who had been pensioned off years ago and continued to haunt the place after he retired, doing odd jobs. He brought me his most cherished possession, a stuffed pike he had caught in his boyhood and which he kept in a glass cage.

The other came from Iris, who brought me a framed photograph, which must have been taken twenty years ago, of David, her and me in an open-air café in Stockholm. We were there on business. Iris called it Golden Days. I suppose it did represent the golden days of my life when I had just broken through from being a small businessman into something rather substantial. Scandawools wasn't Marks and Spencer or Great Universal Stores, but we provided a reliable article at a reasonable price and made more than a reasonable profit, so that I could put my hand in my pocket for this good cause or that and I was becoming something of a figure in business circles. The children were doing well at school, and although I wasn't a believing man, I felt that if there were any outside forces directing our affairs, they were all on my side. Then came Dave's death and suddenly — as if misfortune had been waiting for an opening — everything began to go wrong. We had difficulties with the children. Mother, who though in her late seventies, had been in command of all her faculties (for what they were worth) and had been able to look after herself, became senile and came to live with us. I had difficulties in business. I surmounted them all, but I had two or three black years, and I was not quite the same person at the end of them as I had been at the beginning. I remained eternally on guard. As I said, I was not (and am not) a believing man, but whereas before I had felt that external forces were working for me, I now had the suspicion that they had turned against me and were waiting for a chance to pull the rug from under me. My retirement was their chance.

It was taken for granted, at least by Dora, that once I retired we would move house, but we hadn't decided where. We wanted to be near the children, but not so near — as Dora put it — as to become baby-sitters and home-helps. We had a son and two daughters. The son, Nigel, was an actor. He wasn't so well known that Dora could speak of him as 'my son the actor'. As far as I was concerned he was 'my son the headache', for he could have made a decent living if he had remained at home and had joined me in the business, but he had been everywhere without getting anywhere. He lived in Hollywood, which didn't mean that he was a Hollywood star, and even if he had been, I wouldn't have been too excited about it. Hester, my youngest, whom we called Gypsy, was an amateur actress, and could have been a star if she had wanted to, and for a bit I was afraid that she might be, but she was too intelligent and sensible for that, became a solicitor, joined a well-known firm, married one of the

partners and settled in Richmond. And Phyllis, who was a
year or two older, and a bit like her mother, which is to say,
not too good-looking and not too bright, married a university professor of all things, and lived in Manchester (as a
matter of fact, he was only a lecturer, but Dora always
called him the Professor and Professor he remained).

Dora and Phyllis were very close, but Manchester was not
the sort of place you went to without good reason; it was
certainly not the sort of place you retired to. Hollywood, of
course, was out, and so, a little hesitantly, we began to look
in the Richmond area. I say hesitantly, because Gypsy had
done a little too well, and her husband was that bit too
successful, and although she was a good daughter and
phoned us and visited us and brought us presents, she
inhabited a different world and I'm not sure if she would
have been all that pleased having us round the corner; but
Dora felt otherwise.

'She's our daughter, isn't she? So her husband's a million-
aire. It's not as if you've done so badly yourself. You're not a
pauper.'

'I'm not talking about money.'

'Then what are you talking about? You've got this thing
about Gypsy. She is beautiful and intelligent and talented
and lucky. If you ask me, I think she's fit to be queen, but a
goddess she's not and besides it would be nice to be near the
river.'

And so we began looking, but it was difficult to find what
we wanted, or at least what Dora wanted. This place was too
big, this too small, this too damp, this one had awkward
nooks, this one had awkward crannies, and that one had
noisy neighbours. I needn't have asked myself what I would
do with my retirement: I'd spend the rest of my days looking
for a home.

One Sunday we were visiting my friend Michaelson, who
had sold out a year or two before me and had retired to the
south coast, when we passed a small house and Dora
suddenly shouted: 'That's it, that's the place I want!'

'It's not for sale,' I said.

'Everything's for sale if you offer the right price. Let's have a look.'

We rang the bell, but no one answered, then a neighbour popped her head out of a window.

'I'm afraid Mrs Grigson's not in, if it's Mrs Grigson you want,' she said.

'Is Mr Grigson in?' said Dora.

'Afraid not. He died this morning. Mrs Grigson's at his funeral.'

'There you are,' said Dora triumphantly. 'Fate. This place was meant for us.'

'Mrs Grigson's still alive,' I pointed out.

'Yes, but she won't want a place like this all to herself.' And as a matter of fact she didn't. Six weeks later the house was ours.

It was a neat little place, all on one floor, white walls, green roof, large windows, central heating, small garden in front, largish garden (too large for my talents) at the back, and two bathrooms. I couldn't see why two healthy people living in one house needed two bathrooms. 'It's not as if we're coal-miners,' I said.

'The older you get the more time you spend in the bathroom,' said Dora.

I took it for granted that we would be moving our old furniture into our new place, but Dora said it wouldn't go.

'What do you mean it wouldn't go?'

'It wouldn't go through the door in the first place.'

'Then take it through the windows.'

'It wouldn't go with the surroundings, it's not the right sort of house for our sort of furniture.'

'What do you mean the right sort of furniture? A chair's a chair and a bed's a bed. If they're still comfortable what does it matter? Don't you ever think of the expense?'

'No,' she said, 'I leave that to you, you never think of anything else. I don't know how you ever built up a business, you're afraid to spend a penny.'

'But what's the sense of buying new furniture when you can still make use of the old?'

'Because the old furniture looks drab, sad. It's got the finger marks from three children and four grandchildren, and you're not so tidy that you haven't left a mark or two yourself. And besides you've got the money, what are you saving it for? To leave in your will? Your children are better off than you are.'

'It's not the money, it's the principle.'

'Principle. What you mean is you don't like spending money on principle. Look, if we don't get new furniture we might as well stay where we are.'

'That's all right with me.'

'It's not all right with me. Besides it's too late, for in case you've forgotten we've already sold our house.'

In the end we had what Dora called a 'compromise'. We kept an odd armchair here, a few pieces of bric-à-brac there and replaced everything else.

'That's how it should be,' said Dora, 'a new house, new furniture, a new start, a new life.'

'What was wrong with the old life?' I said.

'Nothing, but nothing goes on forever, and if we had left it any longer it would have been too late.'

'Too late for what?'

'For a new start.'

# 2

The first thing I asked Michaelson (when we eventually got to him) was how he enjoyed his retirement.

'Like a hole in the head.'

'You've got a nice house here.'

'I had a nice house there.'

'A lovely view.'

'It's all right.'

'It's beautiful.'

'Not when you've got all the time in the world to look at it.'

'The trouble with Michaelson', said Dora, 'is that he's treating retirement as if it's a holiday. It's one thing being in a place for a week or even a month, but another to be there for life. You've got to work out a routine.'

And it was this routine which was the most difficult thing. My trouble is that I'm an early riser. I liked to go to the office by car and, to beat the traffic jams, I used to set out before eight, which meant that I was up before seven (it also meant that I never saw Dora before I left in the morning, a matter about which I did not complain). I would be at my desk before half-past eight opening my mail (or I used to before the mail started coming in about eleven). Iris, my secretary, would be in by quarter to, and then it would be work till six or seven or even eight in the evening, depending on what was happening.

I still woke at six-forty, as I did before, made myself breakfast (as I did before) while listening to the radio, and tidied up. And what then? It was still only half-past seven with the streets empty and silent and the whole day stretching ahead of me with nothing to do. I would take a walk along the front, bent double against the wind, which I rather enjoyed, all the way along the promenade, and all

11

the way back, and by the time I got back the shops were still closed, the papers had not yet arrived and Dora was only just beginning to stir.

I would join her in a cup of tea while she was having her breakfast and then read the papers, even the editorials (something I had never done before), but even after all that and after I had helped Dora to clear up, it was still short of ten.

'You could help me with the shopping,' she said.

It took us five minutes to drive over to the supermarket and a further ten to find a parking place. Dora, I discovered (though I should have remembered for we used to go shopping together on holiday), was a discriminating shopper, and she squeezed, prodded and sniffed before buying anything and I was afraid that she might also start haggling. That took the better part of the morning. We then went into a coffee shop, did a bit of window shopping, had a look at the local library and by the time we got home it was one o'clock.

'How time flies,' said Dora. 'The morning's gone.'

It had been the longest morning of my life.

I helped to make lunch and clear up and then came the Great Decision.

My late father gave me one important piece of advice in his life.

'Be careful about a nap after lunch, because once you start sleeping after lunch you're an old man.'

'You take a nap after lunch,' I said.

'I'm an old man,' he said.

He couldn't have been much more than forty, but I thought of him as old, or at least as elderly, even then, and thus, although I allowed myself an afternoon nap at weekends, I would struggle against it on weekdays and no matter how tired I was, and no matter how little I had to do, I never allowed myself to doze off.

'Go and have a nap,' said Dora when we had cleared up and after I had spent ten minutes getting the rubber gloves off my hands.

'No, no thank you. Once you start napping in the afternoons, you're an old man.'

'And what do you think you are — Peter Pan?'

I decided to visit Michaelson. He lived some distance
away and almost without thinking I got into the car, but I
got out of the car and walked. Why not? I had all the time in
the world, and I thought I might as well use my legs while I
still had legs to use, but he didn't seem to be in. I pressed the
bell and pressed, knocked the knocker, banged the door,
but no one answered and I was about to walk away when I
heard a rattling of bolts and chains and Michaelson came to
the door. He was in pyjamas and dressing-gown.

'I'm sorry to disturb you. If I had known you were in
bed —'

'Where the hell do you expect me to be at this time of
day?'

That was an eye-opener. It was one thing to stretch out on
a couch for a nap, but to undress and go to bed right in the
middle of the day! Michaelson was going downhill — unless,
of course, the poor man was ill.

By chance I met him the very next day in the doctor's. As
I said before, I suffered a bit from my bronchials and I woke
up in the morning wheezing and spluttering, and I thought
I'd go along for a prescription. Apart from anything else it
was something to do. I had asked Michaelson to recommend
a doctor.

'They're no good, none of them,' he said, 'but Dr Flecker's
got a better class of patient.'

There were about a dozen people in the waiting-room and
their average age must have been about ninety-five. I found
Michaelson hunched up in a corner reading an old number
of *Country Life*.

'What's your trouble?' I said.

'Kidneys. What's yours?'

'Chest.'

'Chest is nothing,' he said. I wasn't going to start arguing.

'Wait till your kidneys pack up,' he said.

'Have your kidneys packed up?'

'No, but they're beginning to pack up.'

'Did the doctor say that?'

'And if he didn't, do you think I wouldn't know for myself. I've lived with my body long enough to know what's wrong, and besides I've had an examination.'

'An operation?'

'Examination. Operations is old hat. They don't open you up just like that, they shove things up your whatsit.'

'Your what's what?'

'You know I think your hearing is going. Ask to be sent to an ear specialist while you're here.'

'I can hear Dora perfectly well.'

'People two streets away can hear Dora perfectly well. Anyway, as I was telling you, instead of opening you up they shove this thing up your backside—'

'Your what?'

'Your arse!' he shouted. There were gasps and a clatter as several of the patients dropped their walking-sticks. 'They shove this thing up and have a look round. You'd be surprised what they can get up your backside these days. They have one of those stethoscope things they used to have in submarines. Remember all those U-boat films in the war? Achtung, here come ze British pig-dog.'

'They shove a submarine up your backside?'

'Not a submarine, you twit, a stethoscope.'

'I rather think', said a white-haired figure sitting next to him, 'you mean a periscope.'

'That's it, a periscope, and they go whoom! Right up your arse, and they see everything, kidneys, lung, liver, what you've had for breakfast, all from the inside. A pleasant experience it's not—and also you've got to be careful what sort of doctor you've got in case he takes liberties—but it's better than being opened up. Of course, I've also been opened up in my time, but I was a much younger man then and for a time it didn't look as if I was going to get much older, because once you're opened up the devil himself can get in. They weren't sure what they were looking for, but as they thought I was as good as gone anyway they felt free to experiment and began prodding this and cutting that — and I had a drip at one end, and a drain at the other and —'

The doctor was slow in coming and by the time he arrived one or two of his patients had passed out, but whether it was due to the long wait or Michaelson's monologue I couldn't tell.

As we were going out he asked me to join him for a drink. I thought we would go to a pub but he took me to the cocktail-bar of a sea-front hotel. The hotel itself was a bit musty and faded and it looked as if not a living soul had set foot in it in the past twenty years, but the cocktail bar was all tarted up with flashy carpets and wrought-iron and plastic flowers, and a red-haired barmaid with a deep voice who looked and sounded like a man in drag.

We were the only people there and as we sat drinking in a corner Michaelson said to me with a lecherous look in his eyes:

'What do you think?'

'Think?'

He pointed over his shoulder.

'The barmaid.'

'What about him?'

'Her.'

'Her.'

'Doesn't she do anything to you?'

'What should she be doing to me?'

'If you don't know I shouldn't have asked.'

'I don't know what you're talking about.'

'Don't you ever go to the pictures?'

'Sometimes, if I have to.'

'You mean when Dora makes you.'

'When Dora makes me.'

'And what do you see?'

'The same thing whenever I go, which is why I'd rather not go.'

'You mean sex.'

'Call it what you like. People getting into bed, people getting out of bed, people getting on top of each other, none of them with clothes on. You've seen one, you've seen the lot.'

'And they don't do anything to you?'

'What should they do to me?'

'We're back where we started. Don't you ever want to go to bed with another woman?'

I looked at him open-mouthed, for as a matter of fact I didn't much care to go to bed even with my own woman. As far as I'm concerned—and I've been feeling that way for some time—bed is a place to sleep in, perhaps also to read a book, but mainly to sleep in. I'm a good sleeper and I enjoy sleep. When I was a young man and my friends went to this party and that party, sometimes staying out all night, I usually remained at home because no party I had ever been to was as good as a night's sleep. It used to worry my mother. 'You'll never find a wife if all you can think of is sleep,' she said, though when I eventually did find a wife she would rather I had thought of sleep, because Dora was not of very good family (not that my own family was anything special, but then it didn't have to be because I was a boy), but what made it worse was that Michaelson, who was my best friend, had married into the nobility (or so it seemed to my mother). Respectably married men can have many a murky thought—I've had a few myself—and maybe even do a few murky things—but he was seventy if a day, a dried-up little man with white hair who looked like a retired clergyman.

'Go to bed with another woman?' I said.

'Go to bed with another woman,' he repeated. 'You make it sound as if it's never been done before. It's not like climbing Everest, you know.'

'So they tell me.'

He lowered his voice and leaned towards me: 'This one behind the bar is the hottest thing on the south coast, and she's got a friend almost as hot.' Small bubbles began to form at the corners of his mouth as he spoke. 'She hasn't got the same refined build as this one. She's a bit over-blown, but hot—you've got to wear asbestos to get near her. They've got a room upstairs. We could be in and out before you could say Oi vay!—'

I picked up my prescription. 'I'll be late for lunch,' I said.

I didn't see Michaelson for a week after that, maybe two, maybe a month (you lose all sense of time when you retire). It rained most of the time, not real, full-bodied rain, but a sort of grey, wet mist. Skies were grey and the sea was grey and you didn't know where the sky finished and the sea began. My bronchitis got worse and I went to bed hoping I might get pneumonia and a quick end.

'You'll get better,' said Dora, thinking she was comforting me, and as luck would have it, I did, though I didn't feel better. And the rain didn't stop.

'You'll cheer up when the better weather comes,' she said.

The better weather came and I didn't cheer up. If anything it seemed to mock me.

'You don't see nothing of Michaelson,' said Dora. 'You've quarrelled or something?'

'No, we haven't quarrelled.'

'He doesn't come here, you don't go there, it looks like you've quarrelled. Why don't you give him a visit? His wife can't be much company for him.'

I put on my coat, went down to the front and then, after walking back and forward past the hotel with the flashy cocktail bar several times, I went inside. Michaelson was in a seat by the window with a glass in his hand, a glint in his eye.

'I knew you'd be back,' he said.

For the first time I noticed—or did I imagine it?—that his ears were pointed.

3

'He's a new man,' said Dora. 'He didn't want to retire, he didn't want to move. Anything I wanted he didn't want. What'll I do with myself, he kept asking. I said to him don't worry I said, you're the sort of person who'll always find something to do with yourself wherever you are and whatever you're doing. I'm not saying I'm a prophet, but what I said is what's happened. I hardly see nothing of him. He's busy from morning till night. What's he doing? I don't know what he's doing, but what does it matter as long as he's happy? Look, you come down this weekend and if he's not a new man, then I'm not your mother.'

I was in one room watching television, she was in the other talking on the phone, but as Michaelson said, I'd have heard her if she'd been two streets away. I presumed she was talking to Phyllis, first because she'd been going on for the better part of an hour and Phyllis was about the only one I knew who could listen to her for hours without interruption and also because of her relaxed way of talking. She could sometimes be on the phone to Gypsy for an hour at a time but her conversation was always more hesitant, as if she was thinking what she was saying, whereas with Phyllis she opened her mouth and let things flow. Phyllis you could chat to, Gypsy you conversed with. But I was mistaken, it was Gypsy.

'She was worried about you,' said Dora.

'What's there to worry about?'

'That's exactly what I said to her. Anyway she's coming to see for herself. I asked her to bring Nathan.'

She arrived the next evening in a sloppy jersey and a faded pair of jeans looking more like a schoolgirl than a partner in an important firm of solicitors. She looked good in sloppy clothes, as she looked good in anything, but they

18

would annoy Dora. 'She's got a wardrobe full of clothes straight from Paris,' she would complain to me.

'Does she have to put on a Dior gown to visit her parents?'

'No, but she doesn't have to put on one of her husband's cast-off pullovers. Look at the trouble I take when I go to visit her. She doesn't even wash her face.'

'She comes here to relax.'

'No, I'm sorry, it's not good enough. I know we're only her parents, but she could treat us with greater respect. She thinks we're peasants.' (Iris had once remarked that when Gypsy came to see us she acted like the chatelaine of a great estate visiting her peasants and the phrase had stuck.)

Dora's complaints I should add were never voiced in the presence of Gypsy and she fell upon her with kisses as soon as she arrived.

'Nathan not with you?' she asked.

'Does it look as if he is?'

'He couldn't come?'

'Too busy.'

'At weekends?'

'He's always busy.'

'What a pity,' she said, though in fact she was as relieved as I was. She had nothing against Nathan, on the contrary, she was proud of him. More, she went in awe of him, so that when he was around she always wondered if she looked right, or dressed right, did the right thing and said the right thing and in case she didn't, she kept her mouth shut, which was no easy thing for a woman like Dora. He was what she called a catch 'with a capital K', a senior partner in a large firm of solicitors and from an old and distinguished family.

'Your mother used to think your family was something,' Dora used to chide me, 'but you're nobodies, nobodies, compared to Nathan.' His family had lived in England since the seventeenth century and his was the only branch which still remained Jewish. Debrett became Dora's favourite reading from the day Gypsy brought him home and she worked out that he was the second cousin twice removed of an earl with a seat in Wiltshire. The seat was open to the public and I was afraid that when we went on a guided tour that Dora might introduce herself as a relative, but she was a little taken aback when she found the earl himself, a bent, sullen little man in a thread-bare suit collecting the half-crowns as we filed in.

'He could have been a shopkeeper in Hackney,' she said with disbelief. Nathan, himself, however, was every inch the aristocrat, tall, thin, long-nosed and sallow with a bad complexion and black wavy hair and, as Gypsy put it, 'handsome in a repulsive sort of way'. She had qualified as a solicitor and had been working for him for a month when he proposed marriage. He'd been married before and she was his second wife. In a way he was a catch, but somehow I wasn't happy about my Gypsy getting second-hand goods even if they were of top quality. He was also much older than her. Whenever I said that Gypsy could have waited, Dora would answer, 'But look what a lovely house she has,' which she did, with servants (or at least a servant) and two cars and a deep freeze large enough, as Dora put it, 'to take a cow and two horses'. And in order to make good use of it she cooked about once a month, a cow at a time, I think. Big freezer, or little freezer, it would have been nice to have had a son-in-law you could talk to, chat with, gossip with, exchange a dirty joke with, or complain about the way business was doing. Nathan never had much to say, and when he was about, neither did we, and although Gypsy kept asking us to stay with her, the only times we enjoyed doing so was when he was away, and even then we felt he was haunting the place. But the main thing Dora had against him was the fact that he had no children, none by his first wife, to whom he'd been married for about ten years, and none with Gypsy, to whom he had been married for about six.

When Phyllis was married and a year passed without child, Dora lost no time in asking what was happening and about six months later it happened. Three other children followed in quick succession, in such quick succession that Dora began to worry if she wasn't perhaps overdoing it.

That, however, was not the sort of subject which even Dora could raise with Gypsy. She could talk to her about everything else, but not that. It wasn't even that she had been warned off the subject, but she knew what was out of bounds and what was not and she consoled herself with the thought: 'After all she's got a career.'

'And a big freezer,' I added.

Gypsy nearly always came with some sort of present and if the sloppy clothes annoyed Dora, the presents annoyed me, for it created a slight distance between us, as if she was a visitor rather than a member of the family. This time she brought a crate of wine.

We were not really wine-drinkers in our family. We weren't even beer-drinkers. We were lemonade-drinkers, but discerning ones and I knew a good lemonade from a bad and sometimes, on special occasions, I enjoyed a glass of whisky. It was Gypsy who introduced us to wine and even Dora spoke knowingly of Nuit St Georges or Grevy Chambertin, though she drank it with lemonade and fell asleep after a glass, which is exactly what happened this time and it gave Gypsy and me a chance to talk. Come to think of it, that may have been the reason why she brought the wine.

She had been looking at me with what I thought was excessive curiosity throughout supper and when we were clearing up she said to me:

'I don't like the way you look. You shouldn't have retired.'

'Tell that to your mother,' I said.

'Now you're being unfair.'

'What do you mean unfair? Why do you think I retired?'

'Because you wanted to.'

'Because *I* wanted to?'

'Mother's got a nose for weak points, but she won't push where she knows she won't make headway. You found in her badgering an excuse for doing what you've always wanted to do.'

'You've been reading too many psychological books, my girl. I didn't want to retire, believe me I didn't want to, but when I got a pile of money thrown at me on top of your mother's badgering I collapsed. Your mother I could have withstood, and the money I could have withstood, but the two together I couldn't. But what's the use of talking.'

'What did Iris say?'

'She had her own interest to look after. She'd be working for a much larger firm with better prospects for promotion. She had got about as far as she could get with me.'

'And she told you to accept?'

'Of course. She's got her head screwed on the right way.'

'If she'd had her head screwed on the right way, she'd have left you years ago, but of course she's working-class and was perhaps a little nervous of rising above her station.'

'She's not working-class. She's middle-class.'

'Her father was a barman.'

'A publican, and he owned the pub.'

'She told me he was a barman.'

'Now she's doing well herself she likes to think she's from humble origins. He was a publican.'

'Why don't you start another business?'

'At sixty-six?'

'She might join you.'

'Who?'

'Iris.'

'Iris?'

'Iris.'

'Why are you suddenly trying to pair me off with Iris? She wouldn't join me and I wouldn't dream of asking her to. I'm sorry for anyone who hopes to set up a business in this country today, even at twenty-six. Everything's piled up against you, every disincentive, tax, insurance, everything and even then, if in spite of the obstacles you begin to get somewhere, they knock your legs from under you. I'm sorry I retired, but I comfort myself sometimes with the heart-aches I suffered when I was in business.'

'So what do you do with yourself?'

'Read a bit, walk a bit—'

'Rot a bit.'

'A bit.'

'Mother says you're a new man, busy, busy, busy from morning till night.'

'I keep out of her sight—which is one way of killing time. Actually things haven't turned out as bad as I thought. When we first came, there were days I was afraid to walk on the pier, in case I should jump off. I wouldn't jump now, but if someone pushed me, I wouldn't hold it against him.'

'You know what you should do?'

'What?'

She put her head round the door to see if Dora was still asleep.

'Get yourself a bird.'

'A what?'

'A bird.'

'You mean a parrot?'

'Dad, you're not that dim.'

'And what'll that do for me?'

'A man's as young as his next woman. You've been ageing terribly, far faster than mother.'

'And doesn't a woman feel as old as her next man?'

'She might if it was anything permanent, but all I'm suggesting is something that would get you out of the house every now and again. Mother's told me you're busy from morning till night. I've seen no signs of it. You don't garden, you don't play golf, you don't even smoke. A man, as Lady Bracknell said, should have an occupation. Get yourself a bird.'

I put my head round the door to see if Dora was stirring: she wasn't.

'And supposing I told you I had one?'

'I'd say you were a bloody liar.'

'Shows how much you know your father.'

'I know my father.'

And she did.

That day when Dora, much against my better judgement, urged me to go and see Michaelson, I said to myself, well if that's what she wants, then upon her own head be it, and I felt as if I had had a special licence to do something I shouldn't, and I went out with every intention of doing just that, and by the time I got to the hotel I was in a bit of a state. In fact I had surprised myself somewhat to find I could still work myself up into such a state.

'Where is she?' I said to Michaelson.

'Who?'

'You know who I mean.'

'Oh her, it's her day off. She's gone to Brighton with her friend.'

Talk about being all dressed up and nowhere to go? I felt silly and embarrassed. I had shown myself up for what I was (or what I could be) without any benefit.

'Have a drink, calm yourself down, we'll find someone else.' He was obviously enjoying my embarrassment.

'I'm not an alley-cat.'

'Nothing wrong with alley-cats as long as you're not neutered.' And he gave me a dig in the ribs. For a minute — though only that minute — I disliked him. He suggested that we drive in to Brighton for the evening.

'Brighton's full of them,' he said, 'all shapes and sizes, all colours. You'll have the time of your life.'

'No thanks.'

I wasn't suddenly turning prim. I had been in the mood for a moment, and that moment had passed. Besides which, it was one thing having a bit of the other when it was there on your doorstep, but having to drive miles for it seemed a little depraved. I never returned to that hotel again. The very sight of it reminded me of my humiliation. If I could have hired a bulldozer to push it into the sea, I would have done, but still I was glad to have made it up with Michaelson. He was good company when he wasn't salivating about women. I didn't even blame him for salivating about

women. He hadn't had much joy out of his wife, poor man.
She had been a pretty little flower of a woman when she was
young, gay, lively, colourful, but something had happened
to her over the years (perhaps it was Michaelson) and all
spirit had ebbed out of her. I remember after a visit saying
to him: 'Give my regards to your good wife,' and he said,
'give them to her yourself,' and there she was, right next to
me. She was quiet, shy, timid, almost speechless. She
suffered from some sort of complaint to which different
doctors had given different names, but for which none had
found a cure, though she felt better by the sea than away
from it, which was why he had finally retired.

I was still frequently on my own, for Michaelson slept in
the afternoons and he couldn't always go out in the evening,
for his wife couldn't be left on her own after dark, and I took
to exploring the town, especially the part near the old
harbour, which still had a few fishing boats and other small
craft bobbing about.

The day after Gypsy's visit I was by the old harbour
watching one of the boats unloading a catch, when a rather
loud voice said to me:

'Is that where you come to get yours?' I turned round to
find a rather large woman in a brown duffel-coat standing
beside me, with black hair, square jaw, but rather handsome. 'Is that where you come to get yours?' she repeated.

'Mine?'

'Fish. I always buy my fish *straight* off the boat, don't
touch anything else. I'm not particular what sort of fish it is,
as long as it's *straight* off the boat. Same with milk, *straight*
from the cow, and eggs, *straight* from the hen. The more
hands, the more microbes, the less nourishment.'

She was an artist and invited me back to her place, a
terrace house overlooking the harbour which she had converted into a studio. I was impressed by her paintings which
were mainly of boats and fishermen. She made tea and
served it with large, heavy digestive biscuits which tasted as
if they had been made of gravel.

'I only began painting when I was thirty, you know,' she said.

'Oh, so you haven't been painting long,' I said gallantly, but she missed it.

'Twenty years, nearly. Anyone can learn. All it needs is careful observation and control. I give evening classes in the local institute. Of course it's too late to enrol this term, but you could join in September. Unless, of course, you would like private lessons.'

I wasn't sure how she fitted in Gypsy's 'You're-as-young-as-your-next-woman' scheme, but that evening over supper I said to Dora I was thinking of taking up a new hobby.

'At your age?'

'Why not?'

'What sort of hobby?'

'Painting.'

She put her spoon down.

'Isn't that extraordinary.'

'What do you mean?'

'The coincidence. I was only speaking to Mrs Telfer today' — Mrs Telfer was our next door neighbour — 'and she was telling me she's been taking art lessons in the evening institute. You must go, she said, they're marvellous.'

'And are you going?'

'Not now, the term's nearly over, but maybe in September — '

'You could have private lessons.'

'That ambitious I'm not, nor that extravagant. Are you going to have private lessons?'

'I'm thinking about it.'

'It's a nice change to see you so free with your money.'

The next afternoon, without saying anything to Dora, I went for my first lesson.

I had always lived a quiet, sober, sedate life. Even when I was in the army during the war I was posted within a bus ride of where Dora was evacuated with the children, and I was home most weekends. Now for the first time in my life I had discovered excitement. There was something about the mixture of fish and art, of fishermen and artists, which taken together with the long walk and the sea air made me feel light-headed. I looked around at the boats bobbing on the water, the cobbled quays, the seagulls everywhere, and the small terraced houses, and the whole scene reeled a little, and in my excitement I forgot her address. I tried every door in the terrace before I came to the right one. She greeted me with a large welcoming smile such as I had not seen on any face since the children left home (and probably not even before that).

'I've come for a private lesson,' I said.

She leaned over closer to me—she smelt nicely of fresh perfume and fish.

'How private?' she said.


# 4


For the first time in my life I had a secret, not really a guilty secret—in fact it was more of a proud one, and I wanted to share it. But with who?

I had thought of telling Michaelson, but to raise it in the sort of man-to-man conversations we sometimes had would cheapen the whole thing. For this wasn't 'a quick bit of wotsit behind the arras', as he called it. Nor was it 'the real thing', as they put it in films, for I was never sure what they meant by that, but I had the feeling that if I had gone up to heaven and they had stopped me at the pearly gates to ask what I had been doing with my afternoons, and I had said, sleeping with Ada, they would have waved me though.

I thought I would feel grubby, guilty and contrite, but nothing of the sort. In fact I felt clean (though that was perhaps because I always had a shower afterwards). Of course I wouldn't have wanted to hurt Dora, but she didn't know and had no way of finding out. I don't think I acted suspiciously — except sometimes, in fact rather often, when she was talking to me she'd found I wasn't there. Yet I was dying to talk to someone and I suppose those times when Dora found I wasn't there I was talking about it to myself.

One day I had to go to London to see my solicitor and while there I thought I'd drop in and have supper with Gypsy. I found her by herself in her great big house. I have never found large houses happy places. I suppose they need more happiness to keep them glowing than smaller ones, in the way that they need more fuel to keep them warm.

'Aren't you nervous of being here on your own?' I asked.

'We entertain three or four times a week, so being on my own's a pleasure. I wish I could be on my own more often.'

We ate in the kitchen, which was large and chilly with light greens, like an advert for menthol cigarettes.

'Nathan busy in the office?'

'He's in Kuwait.'

'They let Jews into Kuwait?'

'They let Nathan in.'

'Funny, my own solicitor goes no further than Epsom.'

'Nathan's no ordinary solicitor, but look, you haven't come here to talk about Nathan, have you?'

I hadn't, but I wasn't too sure how to begin.

She gave me an amused sideways glance.

'You've done something naughty, haven't you?'

'How could you tell?'

'Lawyer's instinct. I can tell what a client's been up to the moment he sets foot in my office. You've got yourself a bird, haven't you?'

I nodded, feeling oddly embarrassed and proud at the same time.

We were washing up and she gave a loud whoop and threw her wet rubber-gloved hands round me.

'How marvellous. Oh, I am thrilled. What's she like?'

'Biggish.'

'Littleish men do go in for biggish women, don't they?'

'I'm not littleish.'

'Well, averageish. Marvellous.'

'I can't see what you're excited about. I'm being unfaithful to your own mother.'

'Do you feel unfaithful to her?'

'No, but I wouldn't like her to find out.'

'I don't think she would like to find out either. I don't even think she'd mind if she found out, as long as she was sure you were trying to keep it secret.'

'How would you feel if Nathan had a girl-friend?'

'Surprised, but I'm sure he hasn't.'

'That's the way your mother feels about me, and you could be as mistaken as she is.'

'I doubt it, but let's not argue. You know I guessed you'd probably taken my advice as soon as I saw you, a certain look in your eyes, guilt mixed with triumph. You look better for it, you dress better.'

'I always do when I come into town.'

'You don't. Mother says you hate new clothes and that if it wasn't for her you'd still be wearing your demob suit, but you look good, almost handsome.' Her eyes shone excitedly. 'Now come on, tell me, when does it all happen?'

'What do you mean?'

'Do you stay away overnight?'

'Overnight? What do you think your mother would say? No, she likes to fall asleep in front of the television, with me by her side. I can't remember what she did to get to sleep before we had a television, but she drops off as soon as it flickers on. She's a heavy sleeper and I suppose if I put a rug round her and nipped off till the next morning, she'd be none the wiser, but I don't. Apart from anything else I hate to sleep in strange beds.'

'So how do you do it, swinging from the chandelier?'

'I feel this conversation is getting out of hand.'

'It's a natural question.'

'There's certain questions a daughter has no right to ask a father.'

'Does mother ask no questions?'

'Yes, "did you have a nice walk dear?" and I always say with perfect truth yes, though, of course, I don't have to tell her where my walk took me.

'I think she knows and she doesn't know, if you know what I mean.'

'I don't know what you mean.'

'I mean, she doesn't want to know. Most marriages are based on not knowing and not trying to find out.'

'It doesn't say much for most marriages.'

'What I'm trying to say is that people from your sort of background don't like flouting conventions, but can't breathe within them, so they compromise—'

'Where do you see compromises? I don't even know if there are conventions left. I suppose if you're Archbishop of Canterbury you've got to watch your step, but nobody else gives a damn—'

'Are you an Archbishop then, because you're watching your step?'

'What's the point of talking about me, I'm sixty-six, a hangover from the old world—mind you I felt like a hangover when I was fifty-six and probably was.'

'You were born a hangover if you ask me, but the only difference between your generation and mine is that what we treat as of right, you regard as an escapade. I suppose there's more fun in it that way, certainly more excitement. What's her name?'

'Whose?'

'Your mistress.'

'Don't put it that way, you make it sound French.'

'Well girl-friend would sound ridiculous.'

'Say my friend.'

'My friend? Makes you sound like an old queer.'

'Old what?'

'Queer.'

'The older you get the more complicated life gets. You may not believe this, but I'd never even heard of such things when I was your age.'

'You've had a sheltered life.'

'Sheltered life? I was four years in the army.'

'In the quartermaster's stores.'

'And I was a sergeant, you're forgetting.'

She began to sing in her soft, breathless, rather melancholy voice:

'There were queers, queers, who buggered all their peers,
In the stores, in the stores.
There were queers, queers, who buggered all their peers,
In the quartermaster's stores.'

'Not when I was sergeant.'

'No.'

'It was a model unit.'

'You should have been in the navy. Nathan was in the navy.'

'I know he was.'

'An officer.'

'I know he was.'

'And a queer.'

I looked at her incredulously.

She smiled. 'It's all right, I'm only joking. I've got a perverse sense of humour.'

I didn't believe she was joking for a minute, yet I wasn't as shattered as I felt I should have been, but rather confused. Homosexuality was something I associated with people like Oscar Wilde, writers, artists, bohemians, funny men with funny ways who wore baubles round their necks, not with prominent solicitors, and certainly not with my own family. We were all so normal, decent, middle-class, but then, of course, Nathan wasn't. He was from an old family and a wealthy one, and I suppose with older families you had to expect some sort of abnormality.

'But if he's made that way, why did he want to marry?'

'I said I was joking.'

'I know what you said, but you're not answering my question.'

'One has to keep up appearances.'

'Even nowadays?'

'Even nowadays. He's a lawyer, you know, not an actor, with a lot of overseas clients, and overseas clients especially expect conventional behaviour.'

I couldn't quite understand how she was so cheerfully reconciled to her odd situation. Had she no yearning for normal family life at all? Perhaps not. Normal family life was something I associated with Phyllis, with babies and napkins and potties and safety-pins and lotions and talcs and anti-gripe waters. Phyllis had four children in six years, and even after she stopped bearing babies she talked of them and smelled of them and every time she came down for a weekend we were involved in the sort of logistics required to move a small army and there was always something small crawling round her feet, or on her lap or pulling at her hair. Gypsy was perhaps too precious to be domesticated. She was tall and rather dark (hence her nickname), with velvety jet-black hair, soft brown eyes, fine teeth, a long neck, hands which seemed to me a little too long and too thin, a flawless skin.

'Does mother know?'

'No, don't tell her. She wouldn't understand.'

I'm not sure if I did. I had been relieved of one secret, only to be burdened with another.

I returned home comforting myself with thoughts of Phyllis. 'I wish all my children had been like Phyllis,' Dora said to me once, 'simple, sweet, straightforward, uncomplicated, the sort of child you get joy from. The others are headaches and heartaches. Her marriage is what I call a marriage.'

But perhaps it was all an illusion. Perhaps her husband was an hermaphrodite.

5

One evening Dora and I were invited out to our next door neighbours, the Telfers. I hadn't had too much to do with them, but Dora had something to do with everybody and they asked us round for coffee. Dora treated it as something of an occasion and examined my shoes to see if they were properly polished and my collar and cuffs to see they were properly clean.

'Should I put on evening dress?' I asked ironically.

'No, that would be overdoing it,' she said, 'but I don't like the way women have to put on the best of everything and men waddle in in baggy trousers and frayed cuffs.'

We waited till we could hear other guests arriving before we came round ourselves and as we entered the lounge who should be the first person I should set eyes on, but Ada, in a low-cut dress and earrings like small chandeliers. I saw her before she saw me and I had a quick think whether I should mumble some excuse like 'I'm sorry, I've just had a heart attack' and flee, but it was too late. Mrs Telfer was already introducing us.

'Ada, I want you to meet Mr and Mrs Newman, our next door neighbours. They're new to the district. You haven't met, have you?'

'No,' said Ada, looking me straight in the eyes, and I breathed again.

'Ah,' said Dora, 'you must be the marvellous art teacher everyone is talking about. Next September, if I'm alive, I'm joining your class. In fact Sidney, my husband here, was talking about going to you for private lessons.'

'Was he?'

'Maybe I shouldn't wait till September—at my age who knows what could happen till September. Perhaps you can have a class just for Sidney and me. What do you think Sidney?'

Sidney didn't know what to think.

'I don't know if I've got time for many more pupils,' said Ada.

In one way or another, it was a very long evening. There were four or five other couples there, mostly about our age. All of the men had been in the army, all had been officers and had seen action in places like Burma, Assam and Libya. I'd never been further than Basingstoke, and the best I could do was to keep quiet, which was more than Dora— who was obviously having the time of her life—could do. I used to be embarrassed by Dora but it had changed over the years to what Gypsy called 'affectionate exasperation'. It was not so much what she said (and whatever the topic she always somehow managed to bring our children into it), or the way she said it, or even the amount she said, but her tone which, as Gypsy put it, was 'hysteriophonic'.

Ada was surrounded by most of the men—in fact all of them, except me—for much of the evening, and when we came home Dora said to me, 'I had to giggle.'

'What about?'

'All these men sniffing around that tall artist woman. They're barking up the wrong tree.'

'What do you mean?'

'She's a Lizzie.'

'A what?'

'A lesbian.'

'A Lezzie.'

'Lessie, lizzie, you know what I mean. Such a

34

shame. A woman like that could make a man happy.'

'Who said she doesn't?'

'Don't you know what a lizzie is?'

'How come you know so much about all these things suddenly?'

'I watch television, I read. There's more things going on in this world than you and I were brought up to know about. Kathleen knows her—'

'Kathleen?'

'Mrs Telfer. She's been going to her classes for years, she knows her.'

'Is Mrs Telfer a lesbian then?'

'I didn't mean she knows her in that way, but they talk a lot and she knows a lot. You can learn a lot from Kathleen.'

'I can see that.'

The next morning I happened to bump into Mrs Telfer in the supermarket and I said to her: 'That was a lovely party you had last night.'

'It wasn't really a party, just a few friends round for a drink, but I'm glad you enjoyed it. I was saying to your charming wife, now that you have settled in and settled down we must really see more of each other.'

'I wanted to ask you about the art lessons.'

'The art?' And she put up a cautionary finger. 'You're not really interested in the art lessons, are you? It's Ada. She is very attractive, isn't she? There's quite a story there, Mr Newman.'

I hadn't brought the car and she gave me a lift home and I helped her unload her groceries and take them into the kitchen. She was, I noticed, for the first time, really rather an attractive woman, good complexion, without a wrinkle, high cheek bones, grey hair well groomed. She looked a good bit younger than her husband, a sullen, white-haired man who pottered around in the garden with a pipe in his mouth. That morning he was out playing golf.

'You don't play golf, Mr Newman?'

'I save my energy for better things.'

'At your age, Mr Newman?'

'How old do you think I am?'

'It's difficult to say with men, but we're all at an age when we don't think about anything else.'

'Well, I am and I suppose your husband is, but you don't look as if you are.'

'I'm not sure if that's intended as a compliment, but I'll take it as one, shall I?'

She made coffee which she served with McVitie's chocolate digestive biscuits and every bite made me think of Ada and how much her biscuits were better than Ada's.

'Now you want to hear more about Ada, don't you?'

'No, I would rather hear more about you.'

'Me? There's nothing to tell, really. Edwin was in the army, then he was in the War Office and now he's here. I'm an army wife, which tells you everything. I've travelled round a lot, army wives do and the worst thing about being an army wife is the company of other army wives. Their talk is all of promotions, who's going to be made what; the expense of schools and the dishonesty of servants. Everything went missing—whole suites of furniture, sometimes. I'm much happier here, aren't you?'

'Too early to say.'

'I gather you've only been retired a few months. Wait another few—you'll discover new faculties in yourself.'

'I'm already beginning to discover them.' I stretched out a hand and grasped hers.

'Mr Newman, I do think you've got the makings of a dirty old man.'

'Old certainly, but why dirty?'

'Lascivious, is that better?'

'Much better.'

'I think you take me for another Shirley.'

'Shirley? Who's Shirley?'

'Over the road. Don't say you haven't met her. She sleeps with everybody. I didn't ask her round last night, it can be a little embarrassing when most of the men in one room share the same secret—not that it's a secret. She's an ageing nymphomaniac. Very useful for men of their age. It lets them know if their equipment is still in working order. Would you like to meet her?'

'My equipment is still in working order.' I took her hand again.

When I got home Dora was in a tizzy.

'Thank God you're back. I went to the shops to look for you, I didn't know what could have happened. I phoned Michaelson, then Michaelson phoned me. He said he'd expected to see you at twelve, and it was half-past and you hadn't turned up. I was going to phone the police. I didn't know what to think. Thank God you hadn't taken the car, I always get worried when you've got the car. But where could you have been, it's nearly one?'

'It was a nice day, so I thought I'd take a long walk.'

'But how long is a long walk? Anyhow you're here. Sit down and we'll have lunch.'

'Not for me. I'm too tired, I'm going to lie down.'

When I woke up she was sitting by my bed with a cup of tea in her hand.

'You all right?'

'Fine.'

'I was going to call the doctor. For years I've been telling you, have a nap after lunch, but "No" you keep saying, once you start napping after lunch you're an old man. Now you've slept four hours, four hours—and you hadn't had lunch in the first place. You sure you're all right?'

'I've never felt better,' which wasn't quite true, for in spite of the long sleep I felt rather washed out.

As I was leaving Kathleen's, sort of slinking out sideways, looking right and left, as if I'd been doing something I shouldn't (which is exactly what I had been doing) there was a woman outside trying to get her car started, and I offered to help. Well, I didn't get her car started, but I started something else, because the woman in question turned out to be Shirley and as I discovered in a minute everything that

Kathleen had said about her was true, and more, which was why I was home so late and why the only thing I could do when I got home was to stagger into bed.

I slept badly that night, either because my conscience was bothering me, or because I had slept well that afternoon. I wasn't even sure that my conscience *was* bothering me, but I was troubled about something and it was—who was I? Who was this person lying next to my sleeping, snoring wife? Could it be Sidney Newman, father of three, lately proprietor of Scandawools, a good rotarian, a past president of his Bnai Brith Lodge? And if it was, who was the ageing Casanova who had in the course of one morning ravished two neighbours, and who had a mistress twenty years younger than himself? Was I merely an old man in a hurry making up for lost time and lost opportunities—'trying out my equipment', as Kathleen put it, to see if it was still in good working order (which it was—in fact in better order than it had been for years. Did the sea air have anything to do with it?). I had never behaved like this before, not even when I was in the army, when a chap was half expected to behave like this and most people did, but I was too busy in those days, and too tired, for once I had received my stripes I felt as if the whole outcome of the war depended on me. My CO had thought the world of me. I could have stayed on in the army after the war if I'd wanted and made a career of it. I would probably have been commissioned, but I couldn't see Dora as an army wife and to be honest I didn't quite see myself as a regular soldier, not in peace time and I took my bounty and, starting almost from scratch, I built up Scandawools. It was like building up a second family. I made a bit of money while I was at it, but the money was almost less important than the company itself and the people I had working for me. By the time I retired nearly all the new hands in the company were the children of the old ones. There was hardly a married man among them who didn't have a Sidney among his boys, or a Dora among his girls, and if I'd behaved then as I was behaving now I'd have felt I had let them all down. But in any case I never had the time then, nor the energy, to behave like this, perhaps not even the inclinations. And I didn't have much opportunity. Of course, I could have made the opportunities. Michaelson went through five or six secretaries a year—I thought because he was a difficult person to work with, but I could see there were other reasons now, whereas I had Iris almost from the day I started. She had good legs, which sometimes put me off my stride when I was dictating, but she didn't have the sort of temperament which encouraged hanky-panky and in any case, I had the feeling—mainly from the ups and downs in her mood—that she had a boy-friend of some sort somewhere, probably a married man (otherwise, why hadn't she married?). There were pretty little girls, packers and the like, whom I might have kept back for a bit of overtime, but the thought had never even entered my head (hadn't it? No, it hadn't—I looked upon them as my own children, and in fact there was one bright little girl whom I thought far too good for the job and whom I had induced to go back to school). If I had behaved then as I behaved now I wouldn't have been able to look Iris in the face (why couldn't I have looked Iris in the face then and can look Dora in the face now, because Iris had a way of scrutinising my features as I fumbled for words). I didn't feel shame or reproach so much as strange. I wasn't myself, or at least my other self, and I liked the other self, Sidney Mark One rather better than Sidney Mark Two, the Casanova of Crocus Hill.

Perhaps I was more attractive in my middle age (old age, if I was to be honest) than I had been in youth, or perhaps a man gets a new lease of life, new appetites and new vigour before he's finally snuffed out. I didn't think I was doing anyone any harm, but the more people I had to keep in ignorance the greater was the danger that my secret would leak out. I thought I had been safe with Ada at the other end of town, then suddenly she had arrived on my doorstep and if that was not hazard enough I was coveting my neighbours' wives (or they were coveting me, but who was coveting whom was almost beside the point). And only a week or two ago I had been disgusted with Michaelson! I was out-Michaelsoning Michaelson at every turn.

# 6

I spent much of the day indoors, partly out of contrition—I felt I owed it to Dora—and partly because it was pouring, noisy, spluttering rain which rapped on the panes and gurgled in the gutters.

When we were washing up after breakfast she said to me, not, I think, by way of admonition, 'You were afraid you wouldn't know what to do with yourself when you retired, well I don't know what you do do with yourself, but there are some days when I see less of you now than I did in London.' So I gave her a chance to see more of me. I don't think she was cheered by the sight.

We had a large picture window in the lounge which gazed out on similar houses with similar picture windows, all of them opaque with white net curtains.

I had bought some thrillers, the type I used to enjoy reading when I was on holiday, by Micky Spillane and others like it, but somehow I couldn't get into any of them now. I didn't even have the patience to go through the morning paper. I was a man for routines. I had got into the habit of taking a long walk on the front first thing after breakfast, then doing a bit of shopping when necessary and finally round off the morning with a call on Michaelson. I suppose one of the reasons why I was upset about yesterday morning was that I had broken the routine.

I don't know if Ada had waited in for me in the afternoon. I had tried to phone her in the evening, but there was no reply. I suppose she'd thought I'd panicked after seeing her in Telfer's and I was afraid of seeing her again. Maybe I was, except that I wanted to see her again. For that matter I wouldn't have minded seeing Mrs Telfer again.

And as that thought came to mind, she came out of her house wearing a black fisherman's hat and a tightly belted black raincoat. She carried herself well on high heels and had a trim figure for a woman of her age — whatever her age was. You had to take one look at a woman like Dora and you could guess her age within two or three years, but Kathleen could have been anything between forty and sixty. Seen from the back she could have been thirty, for she looked better going than coming. There was something slightly hard about the face; though the very smoothness of her complexion may have made it look harder than it was. All faces harden as they get older, but while some women became leathery, she was becoming like porcelain — a trifle glazed. There she was in her mini, settling in, bottom first, and then pulling in her shapely legs, all delicately done. I had been living next door for two months and had only just begun to notice her. Perhaps that was something retirement had done for me, sharpened my perception.

I picked up a book and tried to read again, but no, I couldn't get into it. Apart from anything else, Dora had launched upon her morning chores, which she did with energy and speed, talking as she went, partly to herself, partly to me and she would break off from time to time to see what I had to say, which was always very little — usually a grunt, but which she always took to be yes, you're right. I wonder what would have happened if I had said no dear, you've got it all wrong. It would have tripped her up for the day. It was strange no matter how fast she worked and how little or much she had to do, it took her a morning to do it.

41

It had taken her a morning to get round our four-bedroomed house in London and took her a morning to get round our one-bedroomed house here. I suppose it wouldn't take her any longer to do Buckingham Palace.

At eleven o'clock precisely, chimed out on a little silvery clock which Gypsy had given us as a silver wedding present, she stopped, washed her hands, made tea and brought it in on a tray into the lounge.

'Do you realise this is the first time you and me have had elevenses together since you retired?'

'I don't remember having it before I retired.'

'You're right, so this is the first time ever. What do you have in the office?'

'Coffee with a chocolate digestive biscuit. Can I have a biscuit now?'

'A biscuit?'

'Chocolate digestive.'

'In which case we had better have it in the kitchen. It's impossible to get the crumbs out of the carpet.'

Dora had a thing about carpets. When the children were small she used to bake a special sort of chewey, non-crumbling cake, which didn't taste very good, but which didn't harm the carpet. Mother had reminded me that Dora was brought up in 'a linoleum home', a house without carpets, which was perhaps why she was obsessed with carpets now. She was a pernickety woman, always had been, but somehow it hadn't irritated me in the same way. That's one of the drawbacks of retirement, you have more time to notice, to criticise and to get peevish — that's why all those cross letters to the *Telegraph* from the south coast on any subject you could mention. I was becoming a 'yours — disgusted — Tunbridge Wells'. I wondered if I got on her wick as often as she got on mine. I supposed I didn't, for I would have heard if I did. Dora wasn't one to hide her feelings and in any case, I didn't have so many quirky little ways.

'The carpets are new,' I said.

'I know they're new, that's why I want us to be careful.'

'I suppose we've each got a good ten to fifteen years to go.'
'If we're lucky.'
'If we're unlucky you mean.'
'Is life so bad that you want to drop dead now?'
'It's not so good that I want to stagger on for ever, but that's not what I'm talking about. The carpets have a good thirty, forty years of life in them — no?'
'If we look after them properly.'
'What I'm trying to say is that we don't have to look after them properly because there's no reason why they should last longer than we do.'
'I don't see what you mean.'
'What I mean is, let's have a ball and have our tea in the lounge.'
'If you want.'
'I want.'
She brought the tray of tea and the tin of biscuits into the lounge and spread out a thick sheet of plastic round my feet.
'What's that?'
'To catch the crumbs. Digestive biscuits have particularly gritty grains. They work their way into the carpet and there's no getting them out.'
'Let them do their worst,' I said and kicked the plastic aside. She sipped her tea silently, not saying a word and when I munched my biscuit it sounded as if someone was walking on gravel. When we finished she went down on her knees with a brush and pan and then hoovered the carpet back and forth, forth and back, about twenty times. The more she went on the more irritated I became.
'Do you want to wear a hole in the bloody carpet?' I shouted. She switched off the machine.
'What's that?'
'It's not the crumbs which are killing the carpet, it's the bloody Hoover.'
She put the machine away without saying a word and was silent for the rest of the morning. So was I. When the phone went, we both jumped.

It was Michaelson.

'Are you coming?'

'It's raining.'

'So are you afraid of getting the car wet?'

'I don't like using the car for these short runs. I like a walk.'

'Then walk.'

'It's too wet for that.'

'Have you started beating your wife yet?'

'What?'

'Have you started beating your wife?'

'No.'

'You soon will.' And he slammed the phone down.

About half an hour later Dora began setting the dining-room table.

'Are we having visitors?' I said.

'No.'

'Then why are you setting the dining-room table?'

'You don't like eating in the kitchen.'

'I didn't say that.'

'Just a minute ago you said—'

'That's because I was irritated with the fuss you were making over the biscuit, but we normally have lunch in the kitchen.'

'We've got a nice dining-room with a nice dining-room table, why not use it? How many more years are we going to get out of it anyway?'

'But it's more convenient to eat in the kitchen, there's less clearing up—'

'I don't mind clearing up.'

'I do.'

We didn't have much to say over lunch either. My not having much to say was nothing unusual, but Dora's silence took a bit of getting used to. She didn't quite look the same with her mouth shut. It was, I noticed for the first time, a rather large and rather sad mouth. Now that was something I had never associated with Dora, sadness. It was as if she depended on a constant torrent of chatter to keep her spirits up. And with her silence every sound seemed amplified, the frying pan being put back on the stove, the clink of fork on plate, the stirring of sugar, the slurping of tea. And the sighs.

She had prepared a mushroom omelette with salad, the sort of lunch I normally enjoyed, but I had no appetite for it now. Neither, by the look of things, did she.

When we were washing up I said:

'If the rain doesn't stop soon we'll be flooded.' She remained silent.

'Look at the road, the drains are full. In another hour the rain'll come into the garden and under the door.'

'What does it matter?'

There was a sound of despair in these words that I had never heard before; it didn't sound as if it could have been coming from her.

In the evening we were watching the nine o'clock news, when she said:

'I'm going up to town tomorrow.'

I turned down the set.

'What was that?'

'I'm going up to town tomorrow.'

'Town?'

'London.'

There was a slightly reproachful tone to her announce-ment, as if she was letting me know that she was going back to mother.

'What made you decide suddenly?'

'It wasn't suddenly. I was going to tell you this morning, but you were in such a mood—'

'*I* was in such a mood?'

'All right, you weren't in such a mood, but I couldn't talk to you—'

'Look, if you want to spend the day in London you don't have to start accusing me—'

'I don't want to spend the day in London and I'm not

accusing you of anything, but I've got to visit a friend in hospital, and I'm thinking of staying over the night with Gypsy, if that's all right?'

'What do you mean if that's all right?'

'Why do you quarrel with every word I say?'

'What do you mean if that's all right, why shouldn't it be all right? Have I ever kept you a prisoner?'

'Can you manage—that's what I mean. I'd leave the food out for you in the oven all ready. All you'd have to do is light the gas. Perhaps you want to have Michaelson over for company, I'll prepare double portions.'

'Look, you go to London. If you want to stay over for a night, stay over for a night. If you want to stay for a week, stay for a week. And you don't have to prepare anything. I can look after myself.'

'What you're saying is you can manage without me?'

'What I'm saying is I'm not a child and I'm not ga-ga, but perhaps if we're going to go on like this it might be better if you took a week's holiday.'

'On my own?'

'With anybody you like.'

I slept badly that night and so did she and after lying silently in the darkness for some hours I said, 'What time are you going?'

'After breakfast.'

'Want me to drive you in?'

'You know I hate car journeys. I'll take the eleven-forty.'

'I'll drop you off.'

'If it's a nice morning I don't mind a walk.'

'You'll have luggage won't you?'

'How much luggage do I need for a night—'

'I'll drop you off.'

I dived under my blanket and tried to sleep, turned this way and that, straightened out my bed-clothes, puffed up my pillows, but remained awake. Dora was on her back, with eyes wide open, staring up at the ceiling as if in a trance.

'I'll go in with you,' I said. 'If you don't like going by road

I'll take the train. We'll drop in to see old friends, and perhaps have lunch together, you, Iris and I.'

'What do you want me for? Take out Iris, she's better company.'

# 7

There was a small car parked by the house when I got back from the station and as I pulled up a tall smart-looking woman emerged in a jeans suit. It takes an elegant woman to look elegant in jeans and I gazed at her in admiration for some seconds before realising with a shock that it was Iris. It was only five or six months since I had seen her last and she seemed transformed. I hadn't seen her in jeans before, she wasn't wearing glasses and she had changed her hair style. She had long hair which she used to do up in an intricate pile at the top of her head and which made her look tall and severe. She had cut it short now, with a simple side parting and it made her look much younger and boyish. Then I remembered Dora's words the previous night—or did I dream them—'Take out Iris, she's better company.' Was this a conspiracy? I didn't say so, but I had an odd feeling that it was, though she assured me that she was on a brief touring holiday and had dropped in because she happened to be passing this way.

'You're lucky to find me here,' I said, 'I was going to go to London.'

She followed me into the house and looked admiringly round.

47

'Isn't Dora here?'

'Gone to London for the day. Let me get you a drink.'

I watched her in the mirror as I was pouring it out. She wasn't at all the same Iris, but then that was maybe because I wasn't the same Sidney. Then I looked again and saw myself and I hadn't changed much, not in appearance. I had gone thinner a bit and looked slight, though not half as slight as I had felt beside Ada (she had called me her bantam). I hadn't shaved that morning, nor, for that matter the previous day and I looked bristly round the chin and throat. It made me look rather tough, I thought, or was it decrepit? My hair was only just beginning to turn grey, which wasn't bad for a man of my age. I knew men twenty years younger who were white—that is if they had any hair left in the first place. In some ways I was a well-preserved man. I had most of my teeth and could read without glasses.

'Lost in admiration?' said Iris.

'What's that?'

'I said you were lost in admiration.'

'No, as a matter of fact I was looking at you in the mirror and thinking how different you looked.'

'For the better I hope.'

'I can't make up my mind. I'm so keen on finding things as they are that any change is for the worse.'

'You've changed, or at least you haven't but you look so different without a jacket and tie. This is the first time I've seen you in shirt sleeves.'

'Did I never take my jacket off in the office?'

'Never—at least not while I was around.'

'No, I was a little in awe of you, so was Dora, and she's no respecter of persons. You've done something to yourself haven't you?'

'My hair?'

'No, more than that. It suits you whatever it is, but I'm not sure what it is.'

'I've had my teeth filed if you must know.'

'Filed?' The idea gave me shivers.

'Don't you remember how ragged and uneven they were? I don't know why I didn't have them done years ago—I know why, I couldn't afford it.'

'Do they pay you so much more than I did?'

'You didn't pay me all that much. I was thinking of leaving after you left and they almost doubled my salary.'

'You should have thought of leaving while I was still there and I'd have doubled your salary. I'd have been lost without you.'

'That's why I never left.'

She kicked off her shoes and settled back on the couch with her legs under her, looking alluring in a way I never imagined she could be.

'Aren't you having a drink?' she asked.

'I don't drink. No, that's not true, but somehow I don't drink in my own house.'

'It's cheaper drinking in somebody else's.'

'I go to the pub, which is even more expensive than drinking at home, but it's just that, though my family's lived here for generations, I'm not yet the sort of Englishman who pours himself a drink when he comes home and I always feel out of it in real drinking company.'

'You were like Banquo's ghost at the annual Christmas do.'

'I dread Christmas and the Christmas do was the bane of my life—'

'I know it was, but you're a spoil sport. You don't really like to see people enjoying themselves.'

'But were they? I know they were making immense efforts to enjoy themselves. I felt out of it, so did David.'

'David was a snob. He hated the smell of beer. He wouldn't have objected if you'd served champagne.'

'The beer was expensive enough and the gin—they went through whole crates. I remember wondering if I couldn't offer an increased bonus instead of the party.'

'And I said they'd take the increased bonus and still expect the party. Christmas is Christmas.'

'Unfortunately it is. If Christ was to rise again and see the way his birthday was celebrated, he'd wish he had never been born.'

'Do you feel the same about Jewish festivals?'

'They're very sober affairs from what I know of them, enough to drive a man to drink.'

She finished her drink as I was talking and I poured her another.

'What about yourself?' she demanded. 'Have I got to finish the bottle on my own?'

I poured a large whisky.

'Now drink it.'

'Give me a chance.'

'What are you looking for?'

'Peanuts, cake, something. I can't drink without eating.'

'Typical.'

'What is?'

'That is. If you go to a party you can always tell the Jews at a glance—they're the people with a glass in one hand and peanuts in the other. I'll have a nut if you find any.'

'Are you Jewish then?'

'By contagion. I nearly married a Jew once, you know.'

'You did?'

'You look surprised.'

'I thought I'd have known.'

'There's a lot about me you don't know.'

'Obviously, but you could have told us. I mean you're more or less a member of the family.'

'Didn't your daughters have any secrets from you? Well perhaps Phyllis didn't, but Gypsy, didn't she have any secrets—*doesn't* she have any secrets?'

'She's another man's wife and entitled to them, but actually I think she tells me everything.'

'*Everything?*'

'I think.'

'That house is full of secrets.'

'Do you think so?'

'Don't you get that feeling, the many rooms, the dark
panelling, the chilly corridors?'

'It's old, that's why, but look, you're getting away from
the subject.'

'You want to know more about my Jew. Do I have to tell
you?'

'No, no, you don't have to tell me anything.'

'But you want to know.'

'No, I'm just curious to learn why you didn't marry him.'

'Many reasons. He wanted to keep me as a dark secret,
which he did for a while. Then, when I insisted that he
make an honest woman out of me — and this was some years
ago, when it was rather important to be an honest woman —
he asked me to convert to Judaism, which wasn't asking
much for I wasn't much of a Christian and a bit of religion
never harmed anyone, but I couldn't go through with it.'

'Why not?'

'The gauntlet of Rabbis, I suppose, and the time everything took. And the discourtesy. I saw first one Rabbi, then
two, then I was brought into a sort of court-room with three
elderly men in black, all of them with short beards, sitting
on a dais, and I felt as little as if I had been brought before
the magistrates for committing a public nuisance, which I
suppose in a way I had, though it was a private nuisance.
Never a word of greeting, not a smile, not a nod. There was
a look in their eyes of hostility mixed with confusion: "Why
does she want to become one of *us*," they seemed to say, "has
she nothing better to do with herself? What is she up to?"'

'What did they say to you?'

'You won't believe it if I tell you. I had to ask them to
repeat it. You're a gentile, they said, and as a gentile I only
had to keep the Laws of Noah to be sure of a place in the
kingdom of heaven, but once I became a Jew I assumed a
whole new mass of obligations and I was putting my soul in
peril. I looked at them to see if they believed it and they
obviously did, or at least if they didn't they kept a straight
face on it. I asked him if he believed it —'

51

'Whom?'

'My fiancé—if I can call him that—we were never formally engaged. I asked him if he believed in it all, and he said "good gracious no". Then why ask me to go through with it? I said. "For the sake of the old woman," he said, and I said I'm marrying you, not your old woman, but of course I wasn't. That's the drawback to marrying a Jew, you marry his whole wretched tribe, lock, stock and mother. Anyhow I was weak—'

'You, *weak*?'

'I'm a different person in different contexts, I suppose we all are. I continued with the charade. I had to take instruction, which I admit I enjoyed, for I was given a sensitive and intelligent teacher, a woman, far more intelligent and sensitive than the Rabbis I may tell you, but I also had to move home and move in with a Jewish family. It wasn't easy, because I was keeping house for a widowed brother, but I moved in with an elderly pair living in North London and that finished it. The Sabbath, as explained to me by my teacher, was something golden, a thing of beauty and a joy for ever and I looked forward to experiencing it at first hand. It was, I discovered, a time of mortification. Perhaps I moved in with the wrong pair, for they were extremely orthodox and from sunset on Friday till nightfall on Saturday, they were half paralysed with fear of doing anything which might breach the Sabbath, and almost anything you did was a breach. Switching on the light, answering the phone, switching on the television, *touching* certain things, like money or scissors, or fire irons. All that I could get used, or I might have got used to, but one Sabbath I opened the fridge to put in a bottle of milk and the woman gave a scream as if I had stabbed her and the bottle crashed to the floor. "You mustn't," she said in a horrified voice, "you open the door and the engine starts moving."'

'Which engine?'

'The refrigeration engine. You open the door and you lower the temperature and the thermostat starts, which begins the engine.' And then there was the trouble with the central heating, for the thermostat starts if you open a door or a window and I had to be careful about that too and then I had to be careful about the length of my sleeves to keep my arms covered and the length of my hem to keep my knees, and if possible my ankles covered, and finally I had had enough. "I can't go on like this," I told my fiancé. "It's only another few months," he pleaded. "And at the end of it all," I said, "will I not be able to open the fridge door on Saturdays, or answer the phone, or—?" "No, it's nothing like that," he said. "It's like taking a driving test. Until you've got your licence you've got to keep the rules, left-hand signals, right-hand signals, never exceed the speed limit, give way to pedestrians, but once you've got your licence you're away." "If that's how it is," I said, "I certainly shan't go through with it. You can marry your mother instead." '

'And what happened then?'

'We decided to wait till his mother died. She was in her seventies then and in poor health, but I said to him, "She'll outlive you yet." And she did.'

'That sounds like the story of my poor brother David.'

'It is the story of your poor brother David.'

I looked at her with disbelief.

'You don't mean it.'

'Does it hurt you to believe that your brother had shacked up with a shiksa?'

'No, no, it isn't that.'

'He was obviously the most precious thing in your family, the golden boy and he told me that he didn't know how you would take it.'

'I'm not religious, I never was. Father was an atheist. Mother became religious and only then after she was widowed. You know very well this shiksa thing had nothing to do with religion. I'd have been delighted if you had married David.'

'It's easy to say that now, but you look upset even at the thought of it.'

'I am upset, but only because I knew nothing about it. I didn't think he would have kept such things from me. I kept nothing from him.'

'Are you sure? You were an odd family, all very close, all very affectionate, all in dread of hurting one another and all leading secret lives.'

'How long did it go on for?'

'Seven years.'

'Seven years!'

'The best years of my life.'

'If only I'd known.'

'What could you have done? You couldn't have talked sense into your mother. I don't know which was her true religion, snobbery or Judaism, perhaps they come to the same thing. She had never got over your marriage to Dora. Can you imagine what a shiksa in the family would have done on top of that?'

'She reconciled herself to Dora.'

'Much later, towards the end of her life, when Dora became her nurse—and even then she treated her like a menial.'

'You know Dora suspected something, well she always suspects something, but this time she was right. I kept introducing David to eligible girls—'

'"Of good family", as your mother put it.'

'Of good family.'

'Which was to say, rich.'

'Not necessarily—and as you know he was fairly eligible himself, good-looking, quite well-off, and ex-officer, but she said I was wasting my time. "He's got a bit on the side," she said.'

'And little did you know that I was the bit.'

'He was a fool, he should have gone abroad and married.'

'And what would we have lived on? He had expensive tastes. You were the earner and he the spender.'

'I would have helped him out.'

'Not then you couldn't—the firm was going through

a bad patch. You were overpaying him as it was.'

'What do you mean overpaying him, he was a partner.'

'That's what I mean by overpaying him. He had no right to be a partner. He had no business judgement, no commercial flair.'

'I think being an officer spoilt him a bit. It made him feel he was cut out for something big. He remained unfulfilled.'

'Strange you should say that. He used those very words about you.'

'About me? I've done everything I wanted. I established a prosperous business. I've built up a family. I've got children and grandchildren. I've been president of this and chairman of that. I count for something among people who count. No, I'm not unfulfilled. I've had no great ambitions, but the ambitions I've had I've achieved. I've always been one of life's non-commissioned officers, only I should never have retired.'

She held out her glass for a refill and I found myself—a little to my surprise—refilling my own glass.

'You did the right thing,' she said, 'You wouldn't have got another offer like that in a hurry.'

'There's more to being in business than money you know.'

'If that's your attitude you should never have been in business. I also began to doubt about selling out when I saw you on the last day, you looked so broken and bent. You'd suddenly become an old man. But you've got over it obviously. You look better than you've been for some time.'

'I don't feel better, or at least I don't feel myself. I don't want to sound narcissistic, but I liked the sort of person I was, I liked the sort of routine I had, the sort of things I did, the sort of people I met. All that's changed and who wants changes at my age? There was a nice established cycle to things, a sort of comforting inevitability and it's all been broken. I'm never sure how one day will end and how another will begin. I find myself doing the oddest things.'

'Such as?'

'You'd blush if I told you.'

'It takes something to make me blush.'

'I don't know how to explain, but I suppose it's the sort of feeling a maiden might get when she loses her virginity.'

She laughed.

'There's nothing odd about maidens losing their virginity.'

'You feel a bit shoddy.'

'Shoddy?'

'There's no other word for it.'

'That's your Jewish puritanism coming out, it was the same with David. What you're trying to tell me is you've got yourself a bird.'

'A bird? It's more like an aviary.'

'Now that's an erotic fantasy.'

'But it's true.'

'And you were such a prim little chap.'

'Why the little? Just because you're a giantess it doesn't mean I'm a dwarf.'

'Your primness adds to the impression of littleness. I just can't imagine you slipping your hand under a skirt. It's such an underhand thing to do and yet—'

'And yet?'

'And yet I did have the feeling looking at you while you dictated letters and stumbled over your sentence that there was a suppressed libido in that compact little person waiting to break out. There was something corsetted about you.'

'Cosetted?'

'Corsetted, repressed.'

'Anyway, whatever was bursting to get out has got out.'

'Good for you.'

'Is it?'

'You look the better for it.'

'But I wouldn't ascribe that to a quick bit behind the arras. You and Gypsy are the same. I don't know, perhaps all women think like that, maybe even all men. The new panacea. Does your head hurt, your back ache, have you fallen arches, housemaid's knee? Is your floating kidney about to sink? Can't you face the coming day? Do you dread the fall of night? Are you depressed? Have you lumbago? Sciatica? Is your age getting you down? Is your bladder waking you up? Are you liverish? Have you got heartburn? Do you suffer from body odour? Are your bowels closed, your lips chapped, your eyes blood-shot? Do you suffer from blisters, bunnions, corns? Do you have wet dreams? There's a cure for them all—fornication.'

'Don't you know a shorter word for it?'

'You don't expect me to use it in your presence, do you?'

At which she jumped from the couch, threw her arms round me and kissed me on the lips.

'You are a prim little man and I love you.' She had taken her shoes off so that I could almost look straight into her eyes. They were green, flecked with brown and gazed at me with fond amusement.

'What's so funny?'

'You are. I didn't know people like you still existed.' She continued with her arms round my neck and I, almost without thinking, put my arms round her waist. She must have stepped back, for the next moment she had fallen back onto the couch, with me on top of her and at the same moment the door-bell rang. I felt like a woman saved from rape. It was Michaelson. He came in, looked at Iris, looked at me and then back to Iris, sized up the situation and was about to flee, when I pulled him back.

'Stay,' I said, 'we're just going to have lunch.'

'The meal you're going to have doesn't call for company,' he whispered out of the side of his mouth and almost dived through the open doorway. I half felt like diving after him.

# 8

Michaelson phoned at four.

'Is she gone?'

'Yes.'

'You're doing all right my boy. I'm proud of you. I take it Dora's away.'

'She is.'

'When'll she be back?'

'Tomorrow. She's spending the night with Gypsy.'

'Marvellous. What do you say we make up a foursome — not in your house, I know what neighbours are, but we could all have a night in Brighton, a ready bit of you-know-what, something to keep you warm in your old age.'

'But I told you she's gone.'

'All right then, get hold of her. We'll have a bite to eat, then go to the casino and then — on second thoughts why go to the casino? On third thoughts, who needs a bite to eat?'

'I don't know how to get hold of her.'

'What do you mean? Is she somebody you picked up from the street?'

'Did she look like someone you pick up from the street?'

'Depends in which street you do your picking up.'

'Didn't you recognise her? My secretary.'

'That long toothy thing? Get away.'

'She's had her teeth straightened.'

'And did she have her legs shortened?'

'She was sitting down if you remember.'

'From what I remember she was lying down. When I go in for that sort of thing I draw the curtains in the first place and I don't go in for them in my own house in the second.'

'Are you phoning to give me a lecture?'

'I was phoning to say "maazeltov" and I'm suggesting that you get hold of her and that we have a night —'

'And I'm trying to tell you that I can't get hold of her because she's touring,' and almost added that I wouldn't get hold of her even if I could.

'I'll tell you what, come round here for supper.'

'It's too much bother for your wife.'

'What do you mean too much bother, didn't you know she's inside again?' By which he meant she was in a nursing home, though he made it sound as if she was in prison. I asked him to have supper with me.

'Dora won't like it, I make crumbs everywhere.'

'Dora isn't here.'

'But the crumbs remain long after I've gone.'

'Let me worry about the crumbs.'

'What have you got?'

'What do you want?'

'I've got trouble with my teeth. Have you got a bit of liver?'

'I'll find a bit of liver.'

'And maybe a tin of asparagus soup—the tinned stuff mind you, I can't stand real asparagus soup.'

'I'll get some.'

'And maybe an avocado pear to start with.'

'And perhaps crepes suzettes to finish with.'

'Greps what?'

'Blintzes.'

'I don't mind blintzes, cheese blintzes. Will I bring round some beer, you don't keep beer in the house do you?'

'I've got some beer.'

'Do you have McEwan's Export?'

'I don't know, all beer looks alike to me, and tastes alike.'

'I thought as much. I'll bring some round.'

I was glad of his company, but I wish he had stayed when he came earlier in the day. I was afraid when Dora went for the day that what could happen would happen. I particularly didn't want to make love. 'Make love,' what a daft expression, as if it was something like making tea. Love was about the last thing that came into it. Sleeping is a bit more like it, but even that is a misnomer, for if there is one thing you have to be for this sort of thing it's awake and of my four recent experiences only one was in bed. 'Carpetted' was a bit nearer the mark, or 'couched'. Anyway, whatever the word for it, I wished I hadn't done it.

With Ada I had had no crisis of conscience. I had done what any man in my position would have done and almost anyone not in my position would have liked to do. There had been something slightly novel and fresh about the whole experience and I had felt the better for it. Now the whole situation was getting out of hand. It was getting to be something of a dirty habit, like smoking, except that I had been able to give up smoking, while it didn't look as if I could give this up, though in some ways it was more dangerous (when I saw Shirley getting into her car earlier in the day I thought to myself—that packet should carry a government health warning). It was getting to the point where I was having an affair with every woman I met— except my own dear wife. Had I suddenly become irresistible or had I stumbled upon a particularly sex-starved strata of womanhood? The fact remained that I was getting to be afraid to be left on my own.

'I got a theory', said Michaelson, 'that women have a second flowering about the age of fifty before they dry up for good.'

'And men?'

'They flower all the time, but with women this second flowering I must tell you is more exotic and exciting than the first. Of course when I was a young man I was too busy making money to have much time for women, but now that I'm only busy spending it I can take them up as a calling.'

'From what you told me you always had time for women.'

'Yes, a half hour here, an evening there, but never to take it seriously. I used to enjoy a read, but I've got trouble with my eyes. Television gives me headache. I don't get much pleasure from food because my grinders are giving way. You get to an age when the only thing you can enjoy are women—'

'And when you get past it?'

'Then you can start being pious and good. It's the consolation for old age is sex, it's wasted on the young. Of course you need a bit of physique, but not too much as long as you keep in training and keep the bowels clean.'

'What have the bowels to do with it?'

'They interfere with the lines of communication if they're clogged up. The other thing is when you get to my age and yours you can't go in for any of the fancy tackles—'

'Speak for yourself.'

'You go in for the fancy tackles?'

'I'm not your age.'

'What do you mean you're not my age—you're a year or two younger than me, if that.'

'I'm sixty-six.'

'Only sixty-six?'

'How old did you think I was?'

'Seventy, maybe more. When I saw you in the doctor's that day I thought my goodness, he's on the way out. You couldn't even hear properly.'

'I was suffering from retirement shock.'

'You're over it now.'

'I haven't got over it, I'm hardened to it.'

'You mean you've found yourself an occupation. But if you don't mind my saying so, you take chances. I mean Dora could have walked in on you this morning the same as I did.'

'Dora's in London.'

'She could have missed the train.'

'I put her on the train.'

'She could have remembered something she'd left at home and got off at the next station.'

'It was an express.'

'She could have pulled the communication cord. Look, you can never take chances with wives, they can turn up at the most awkward moment. Besides these things always leave traces, I don't mean crumpled cushions, or lipstick on the tumblers, but in the air, like unseen cobwebs and a woman can always sense them when she walks into a room. Even my wife, who, you might think was non compos mentis—well she is non compos mentis—but she has sense enough for that.'

He had me worried.

'How long does it take to clear?'

'About twenty-four hours, if you leave the windows open.'

I got up and opened the windows.

'Mind you, of course, Dora might be broad-minded and why not, she's got a broad everything else.'

'I don't insult your wife, Michaelson, so don't you insult mine.'

'My wife? She's too much of a *nebbich* to insult. She's inside again, you know.' And he gave a long sigh, which almost seemed to deflate him, for he suddenly became a sad and shrivelled little man.

'She'll be out soon," I said.

'I know she'll be out soon, but for how long? She's out one week and back the next. They've tried everything, drugs, electric shock, hypnosis. She sometimes gives little flutterings of life, like starting the car on a cold morning, but never really gets moving. Do you remember what she was like as a young girl? Big eyes, white teeth, long hair, like an illustration from a children's fairy book.'

'She looks happy inside herself.'

'You mean that daft smirk on her face? Who knows what goes on inside her, if anything. I'd have put her out of her misery years ago, but then who'd put me out of mine?'

The door-bell rang and we both jumped. Callers were rare at this time of the night. It was Mr Telfer, a lean, dapper figure, white hair, white moustache, double-breasted blazer with brass buttons, suede shoes.

'Am I a nuisance?'

My brain raced. In what context? Could he have meant that he was standing between me and his wife? Was he being sarcastic? I had never been 'the other man' before. Would he horse-whip me? Would I have to fight a duel? Where? On

the beach? With what weapons? I knew how to handle a
rifle, but not with any accuracy and in any case they didn't
use rifles in duels, or did they? Was it a criminal offence to
have it off with one's neighbour's wife? I was still Jew enough
to know it was a religious offence. Would my name be
dragged through the courts? I could already see the head-
lines: PENSIONER CAUGHT IN SOUTH-COAST LOVE
NEST. '"I did it to pass the time," said sixty-six-year-old
Sidney Newman, father of three.' Would I be cited as co-
respondent in a divorce case? ' "I'm standing by my husband," said sixty-six-year-old Mrs Dora Newman, wife of
South-Coast Casanova . . .'

'I'm sorry,' I said, 'I didn't catch that.'

'Am I a nuisance coming at this time of the night? Seems
silly to phone people living next door, what? To the point.
British Legion.'

'Pardon?'

'British Legion. Wife tells me you're an old soldier. Surprised you haven't joined the local show. Splendid club
room. Good company. Marvellous bar.'

'Can I join?' said Michaelson, 'I was in the Home Guard.'

'Anyone can, provided he wore the Queen's uniform.'

'The way it fitted, I probably did.'

'You know where it is. Back of the station. Splendid club
rooms. Good company. Marvellous bar. Bags of parking
space. Getting on a bit some of us. Dying, that sort of thing.
Couple of chaps died this morning, or was it yesterday? Lose
all sense of time. Don't suppose it makes much difference to
them. Once you're dead, you're dead. Used to be our regi-
mental motto — unofficial, of course. Official one in Latin.
Came to much the same thing. Not too difficult to bowl a
man out in his eighties. Wickets flying right and left.
Monthly bulletins full of obituaries. Didn't know half the
chaps were alive till I heard they were dead. Yes. Billiards.
Bridge. Marvellous club rooms. Splendid bar. Try it. Avoid
Fridays. Ladies' night. All right, but not the same thing.
Got to watch what you say —'

'And you don't get much chance to say it,' added Michaelson.

'Ah, you've been?'

'No, but I can imagine.'

'Of course some of the wives are old soldiers in their own right. Makes no difference you know. A woman's a woman. Good library, by the way, if you like that sort of thing.'

We had by now moved out of the hallway into the lounge.

'Can I get you a drink?'

'Shouldn't really, but I will. A whisky if you have it.'

I poured drinks all round and we all stood there looking into our glasses as if something desperately important was going on inside. Then Telfer looked up.

'Ever tasted Burmese whisky?'

'No.'

'Poison.'

Silence.

'I once had Spanish vodka,' said Michaelson.

'Spanish, eh?'

'Spanish.'

'Any good?'

'Poison.'

'Yes. Shouldn't imagine Russian sherry is much better,' and we all cackled with laughter. 'Well, mustn't stop.' At the door he turned and scratched his head. 'Came for something, I'll be damned if I can remember what.'

'British Legion?' suggested Michaelson.

'British Legion?'

'Yes, back of station. Splendid club rooms. Marvellous bar.'

'Ah, so you've been?'

'No, but I'll come.'

'Good. Avoid Fridays, though. Ladies' night. All right, but not the same sort of thing. Bags of parking space.'

# 9

Dora was a little subdued when she came back from London the next day and looked tired and strained. I asked if everything was all right.

'Visiting friends in hospital is no pleasure,' she said. 'She was lying there white as a sheet and tubes here and drips there, more dead than alive and hardly able to speak. Anyway I did the speaking for her and I cheered her up a bit, poor Sarah, though by the time I'd finished I felt ready for a hospital bed myself. The place was like an oven and what with the heat and the smells I nearly passed out.'

'And then I suppose you were up half the night talking to Gypsy.'

'No, I hardly had a chance to talk to her at all. She had a dinner party and what a party, a state banquet with ambassadors and ministers and famous people even I had heard of. Everyone was in evening dress and Gypsy, I must tell you, was like a queen, a queen. She was wearing an odd dress, like a thousand chiffon handkerchiefs all stitched together. On anyone else it would have looked like a heap of tatters, but on her—I couldn't stop looking at her, neither could anyone else. She has two Philippino maids and they both kept saying to me, "She your daughter? She your daughter?" as if they couldn't believe it and to tell you the truth I couldn't quite believe it myself. And they had all the silver out—Nathan's family silver, centuries old, priceless—and all the crystal. It was like a scene from a film. And they had a small band you know, not like for a wedding, not for dancing, fiddles.'

'And did you join them?'

'Me join them? How could I join them? Was I dressed to join them? I helped out in the kitchen, but I could see it all and it all finished late, which is why I'm a bit tired.'

'Didn't Gypsy talk to you at all?'

'Yes, for a minute or two after everyone was gone. She was exhausted, poor child.'

I had an odd feeling that something Gypsy told her had upset her. Could she have told her what she had told me? I doubted it. Dora wouldn't have known what to make of it, but why not . . . After all she knew what a lezzie was, even if she didn't know how to pronounce it. Who didn't know what a queer was these days? You hardly heard about anything else, so much so that I sometimes felt that people like me and Michaelson were in a minority — supposing, of course that Michaelson himself wasn't queer, because that barmaid he yearned for didn't look much like a woman to me. 'Everyone's queer, except me and thee, my dear, and even thee's a little queer.' Perhaps that's why every woman I met prostrated herself at my touch. I was the last living heterosexual on the south coast, or at least the last one still on active service.

The following week Dora said she was going to town again.

'Whom have you got in hospital this time?'

'Can't I go to town without visiting the sick? I've got some shopping to do, though as a matter of fact if I have time I'd like to pop in to see how Sarah's getting on.'

'From what you've told me Sarah might have passed on by now.'

'Heaven forbid. She's been through the sort of thing before — several times. But look, can't I go to town without your permission, what's happening here?'

It was a fair question, but I could not give the honest answer which was that I was anxious not to be left on my own, at least not for the time being. There was Kathleen next door, Shirley over the way, Ada by the harbour and Iris in the wings. It was no joke.

'I'll drive you in,' I said.

'To the station?'

'No, to London.'

'What for? I feel safer by train. I don't like you making

long journeys by car, you know that. I don't even much like you making short journeys.'

'I don't know what you're worried about. I've never had an accident in my life.'

'Then there's all the more chance you might have one. Arthur's worked it out, he should know.' (Arthur, Phyllis's husband, was a mathematician.)

'Look,' I said, 'Arthur's had three or four accidents, so by his calculations he should never have another, would you let him drive you?'

'That's another matter.'

'I can't see the point of my keeping a car at all.'

'Nor me. I wish you'd sell it. I'd sleep better at night if you did.'

She had some sort of crazy premonition that I would have a serious car accident one day. She didn't say so, but I know she did, and I admit it made me a little nervous, though it never stopped me from using the car.

'All right,' I said, 'I'll come in with you by train.' She looked a little nonplussed, I thought, but recovered herself quickly.

'All right, if you want, but what'll you do while I'm seeing Sarah?'

'Visit friends, go up to Scandawools maybe. If you want I'll take you out to dinner.'

'Take *me* out to dinner?'

'Why not?'

'What's the occasion?'

'You need an occasion to have a meal?'

'You've never taken me out to dinner just like that before.'

'I've never been retired before.'

'You're being ridiculous, Sidney. At our age we've got to watch it. I've got to watch my figure, you've got to watch your money. It's a waste. We could have a bite at Gypsy's. Besides, she's expecting me.'

'We could go to the theatre.'

'You're forgetting, we've been, just before we left

London, remember? All naked bottoms and dirty words.'

'That was only one play in one theatre. There are a hundred theatres in London.'

'Kathleen goes to the theatre nearly every week and she says they're nearly all the same—dirt.'

If I was a suspicious man (which I'm not) and if she wasn't Dora (which she was) I would have thought she was meeting a boy-friend, a ridiculous thought maybe, but was it any more ridiculous than the fact that I should have three or four girl-friends? In any case she was obviously desperately anxious not to see me in London, at least not till late in the evening. I had half a mind to send a private detective after her, but I parked the car in the station, bought a ticket and travelled in with her.

It's quicker by rail but it didn't seem to be quicker travelling in with her, for her tongue didn't rest for a minute till we reached Victoria.

'It's not so bad now, is it?' she said. 'Retirement, I mean. We started off in the worst possible time, winter I mean. Rain, cold, wet, long hours indoors. But now the weather's getting milder and the days longer, we can begin to enjoy it a bit. We can start on the garden. We can have friends down for weekends. I know Phyllis and the children are dying to see us. I've hardly been out with you at all. I don't like walking in cold weather and you've been out on your own mostly, or with Michaelson, but now it's spring nearly, we can go out more. We can entertain more. We have that lovely terrace and awning at the back, we haven't used them once yet. We could have a barbecue in the garden and the children here and the grandchildren. I can tell you, you'll be asking yourself why you didn't sell out years before . . .' And so on in this vein for the better part of two hours and it isn't that she said anything silly or annoying, but she said it in a voice which made it impossible for anyone in the carriage to do anything but sit up and listen. I can usually switch off when she's talking, but when there are others within earshot, I am kept attentive by embarrassment. The train was non-stop otherwise I would have got out at the first station. As it was I felt tempted to move to another carriage. I didn't know why I didn't.

We arranged to meet at Gypsy's at eight. It was now just after twelve. I had never been in the West End in the middle of a working day for years and I wasn't quite sure what to do with myself. On an off chance I phoned Iris and she suggested that we meet in a Bloomsbury hotel for lunch. She was dressed in a dark-brown tweed dress with a long cardigan and was rather more like her formidable self, though again she wasn't wearing glasses. Perhaps she had invested in contact lenses. She was obviously pleased to see me.

'Guess who phoned me five minutes ago?' she asked.

'Who?'

'Your wife.'

'Dora?'

'How many wives have you got? She wanted to know why I never come to visit you and I almost blurted out "But I was only there last week." I take it she doesn't know I called.'

'Of course not.'

'Why the "of course"? There's nothing unusual in a secretary visiting her former employer.'

'But there was more to your visit than a visit, if you know what I mean.'

'I wasn't suggesting you told her that we'd had it off on the carpet . . .'

There was a crude streak in her which I hadn't noticed before and I almost blushed. Perhaps I did blush, for she broke off.

'I'm embarrassing you, aren't I?'

'A bit, but that may be because I've already had an embarrassing morning. I travelled up with Dora in a crowded carriage to Victoria and her voice, if you remember, does carry.'

'Would you like me to come down for a weekend?'

'Would you like to come?'

'That means you wouldn't like me to come.'

'It would be difficult. I would want to do things which I couldn't if Dora was around and, of course, she would be around. Moreover, she's not stupid—you mightn't think so listening to her, but she's not and she can tell when I'm pining for something. We don't talk very much, at least she does, but I don't, and I don't really have to, because she can read me like a book. I'm not saying she knows everything that goes on inside me—I'm not sure that I do myself—but if she was to be with us under the same roof for any length of time, she would know that something had happened and that given half the chance it might happen again.'

'Even if we behaved with circumspection?'

'Even if we behaved with circumspection and I'm not sure that we would.'

'It takes two to misbehave.'

'But it only takes one to start off the other. No, I'd rather not risk it, or at least not until I feel more settled and myself. Half the time I don't know who I am or what I'm doing. In any case, you know very well I feel embarrassed with Dora when strangers are around.'

'I have noticed.' There was silence for a moment, then she said. 'Can I ask an impertinent question?'

'Why did I marry Dora?'

'I wouldn't have put it as crudely as that, but why did you? It's not as if she even had money.'

'What's money got to do with it?'

'Everything. I've lived and worked among Jews all my life and money comes into everything they do.'

'You know, you're an anti-Semite.'

'I'd be entitled to be one if I was, but you know it's true. You told me yourself how your father put his business into hock to marry off his ugly sisters.'

'I never said they were ugly. They were stupid and plain.'

'But made eligible by money.'

'Don't Gentiles ever marry for money?'

'They do if they can, but it takes a Jew actually to invite tenders. What sort of creatures could he have bought?'

'Hard-up creatures, who as a matter of fact made perfectly good husbands. What should he have done with his sisters, set them up in a house with a dog, a cat and a canary, like your English maiden ladies? It may show that marriage means everything to the Jew, but not money.'

'Why was your family so unhappy about your own marriage?'

'Not because of money. My family was olde English, not very olde — not like Nathan's — second, third generation. We were well established and lived in a large house in Brondesbury Park. Dora's family were working-class immigrants, who lived in Hackney and still spoke Yiddish —'

'I can assure you if they had been middle class and prosperous it wouldn't have mattered where they came from, when they came, where they lived and what they spoke. Whatever their difficulties they would have been made good by money. I remember your mother —'

'You keep going on about my mother.'

'She was perfectly candid.'

'But she could also be stupid. You see, you've never grasped the position of the male in the Jewish set-up. Being male is a form of social standing in itself and the sons are expected to raise the social status of a family. It is usual among Jews for a boy to marry the boss's daughter. Here the situation was reversed and the girl married the boss's son, which is what upset mother, but Dora was no ordinary girl. Do you remember what she was like before she became shapeless?'

'Very well, lively, pert, alluring — in a barmaidish sort of way — slightly tarty, actually.'

'Tatty?'

'Tarty. Over made-up and over-dressed, an eyeful I admit, all work stopped when she came into the warehouse, but it didn't last.'

'The children came, so it didn't last.'

'She's still got something of her pertness, you know, and

with all her shapelessness, a slightly flirtatious quality. This
may surprise you, but men still look up when she enters a
room.'
'That's because they hear her coming.' She laughed.
'She wasn't always like that, if you remember. She got her
loud voice from looking after your deaf mother.'
'My mother grew deaf from her loud voice, but let's not
argue.'
'When I first saw you together I thought she wasn't at all
your type. You were a man of some education, well-read,
articulate—except when you tried to dictate a letter.'
'I was put off by your legs.'
'So you keep telling me, but you never laid a finger on
them, not even in the mini-skirt days.'
'You never went in for those little skirts.'
'I would have looked damned silly if I had, but I always
left plenty of room for manoeuvre even with the new look.
David got his hand in the very first day.'
'Officers' privileges. I was an NCO. Can we take a room
upstairs to make up for lost opportunities?'
She looked at her watch. 'We'll have to be quick.'


# 10


I woke up in a darkened room with a crumpled bed on one
side of me, not quite certain where I was, what time it was,
or even what day it was. This was rake's progress with a
vengeance. It was one thing to mess about with a neighbour's wife in a neighbour's house, but there was something

rather shoddy about resorting to a cheap hotel (the appointments were cheap; the actual costs weren't, but I hadn't been in a position to haggle). I couldn't look the reception clerk in the eyes and it was Iris who booked the room, and I paid for it with eyes averted. Then the hurried walk to the rickety lift, which seemed to creak and groan and — or did I imagine it? — tut-tut with disapproval; the spring along the worn carpet to the room itself, the fumbling in the lock and finally the dive into bed.

'I've an appointment at three,' said Iris as she pulled her clothes off, which put me off my stride altogether, for I am not a man to be rushed. Finally she grew impatient, pulled her clothes back on and left without a word.

For my part, I was weary with the effort, but as I had paid for the room in any case, I went to sleep. I was asleep after lunch — an old man. There were extenuating circumstances, but I was an old man.

I looked at my watch. It was nearly four. I had a further four hours to kill before meeting Dora. I wished I hadn't come into town. For a moment I hated Iris. She had made me feel awkward, feeble, small. She might have said something before rushing off. I had seen her in a temper before, but not of course in such a situation, her tight-lipped face, the angry rustle of clothes, the silence. She might have said something, if only 'good-bye', or better luck next time. I wasn't one for a quick bit behind the arras like Michaelson. I took a certain pleasure in driving at speed, but in everything else I liked to take my time. I wish she hadn't called and I hadn't phoned and I particularly wished we hadn't gone upstairs. Eighteen pounds the room cost me. From what I remembered of my army days chaps paid two bob for that sort of thing, with no one eyeing their watch and telling them to get on with it. She was coarse, unfeeling, vulgar. I even began to wonder if she had really been the family friend I thought she was and a host of little incidents, each insignificant in itself, came to mind to add to my suspicions. And she could be impertinent. I resented her questions about Dora and her remarks about Jews. I was half joking when I said she was an anti-Semite, but I was no longer sure it was a joke. And she could be peevish, as she had been now, like a child denied a half-promised treat.

If this was the end of a perfect friendship, then it was all to the good. I had been uneasy about the way it was developing. In fact I had always been a trifle uneasy in her company. Perhaps it was her size, but whenever I came near her I had the odd feeling that I was about to be swallowed. Perhaps poor old David had felt the same, which was why he delayed and prevaricated and gave all sorts of excuses for not marrying her. If this was the sort of feelings she instilled in me as an ex-secretary, what would she have been like as a wife?

I dressed, feeling grey and dejected. I had thought of dropping in on Scandawools, but I couldn't now and in any case I wasn't all that sure if anybody would be interested to see me. Nobody, with the exception of Iris and old Leslie (who had sent me spinach from his allotment) had bothered to keep contact with me. They had a new governor, new circumstances and the old one was forgotten. If I came among them now it might even embarrass them, like the ghost of a dead husband come to haunt his widow's new ménage.

I decided to go to Mill Hill instead. Our first house after we married was in Cricklewood, our second was in Mill Hill. It was there that the children grew up and went to school and it was there, I suppose, that I had the happiest, certainly the most fruitful, days of my life. Coming back to the place after a day in town was like arriving in the heart of the country, though it was only about ten miles from the centre of London. It felt the same now. The winter was almost over. The air was soft, even though it was only the end of February. The ground was moist. Violets and crocuses were in flower and here and there the closed head of a daffodil was threatening to open.

It was a detached house in its own substantial garden,

with dark, mock-Tudor timbers and lead-latticed windows.
We had four bedrooms and a large attic which Gypsy had
cleared and converted for her own use and to which we were
almost forbidden access.

Nigel and Phyllis had bedrooms on the first floor which
looked like bedrooms and weren't used as anything else.
Gypsy called her room a studio and it was plastered with
travel posters and slogans and littered with books and
musical instruments and uncouth young men would march
through the house to her attic without even nodding 'hullo'
and Dora raised no objections as long as they were careful to
wipe their feet on the mat. Gypsy lived her own life even as a
teenager. We loved all our children equally, but it was
accepted even by Nigel and Phyllis that Gypsy was special
and had to be treated differently, but Dora was a little
troubled by the attic arrangement. She didn't like the
thought of an untidy space at the top of the house and I
think she was a little relieved when Gypsy, who was by then
in her final year at University, asked if she could have her
own flat in central London.

I didn't know who had bought our house. I didn't even
remember the name on the contract, but whoever it was
obviously had money to burn, for we had left the house in
mint condition, the wiring, the plumbing, the drains, the
woodwork, the brickwork, expertly maintained. All the bedrooms had built-in furniture. Dora had a mania for building in, it saved space, she said. She would have had a
built-in piano if she could (and nearly did). The kitchen was
fitted. The bathrooms were fully tiled and had the latest
appliances, but builders were in and they were pulling the
place inside out. I watched them sadly and resentfully.
What was so wrong with the house that they had to change
it? Their entire effort seemed to be a reflection on our taste.
I thought we had a lovely home, everybody said so. It was
certainly a comfortable home (or it would have been but for
Dora's never-ending war on dust) and here they were
eliminating all our traces and with a speed that I had not

noticed among any builders that I had ever employed, as if afraid that somebody might step in and stop them. I should have liked to stop them myself. They were erasing my past. I felt like coming back under cover of darkness and putting a blue plaque on the wall: SIDNEY AND DORA NEWMAN LIVED HERE. 1950-1976.

Twenty-six years! It seemed like yesterday. I was married at twenty-eight and till then each year seemed clearly defined, but from the day I married things quickened to a blurr. The war. My call-up. Aldershot. Basingstoke. VE Day. Demobilisation. Scandawools. And whoosh, before I knew it I was an old man and retired. There were, of course, the children. Somebody once said to me that children were a slow-motion replay and you could see your life all over again by merely watching them, but the children were different from Dora and me in every way—appearance, manner, style, outlook—and they seemed to grow up almost while my back was turned, specially the girls. One day I was collecting them, all fancy ribbons and frilly knickers, from parties and the next I was walking them up the aisle.

I suppose if they had been troublesome the time would have passed more slowly, but even Nigel, who was troublesome, was grown up and away before I quite knew what was happening. But then he wasn't really troublesome. He was a disappointment. I had hoped he might come into the company which I had after all built up into a flourishing concern and which he might have built up into something larger (for I am somewhat cautious and was nervous of growing too fast). He used to work in the warehouse during his school holidays and dismissed the whole concern as a 'twopenny-halfpenny outfit'. I then hoped he might go into the professions, for he was rather bright at school. He could have been many things, but it never occurred to us he might be an actor, for apart from anything else he was slightly mis-shapen. One didn't notice it, for he had tremendous colour and personality—he reminded me a little of his mother when I first met her—and he always seemed to be surrounded by the most attractive girls, but he's shorter than me and much more robust, with massive shoulders and a large head (it took two surgeons to deliver him and they nearly killed poor Dora). I remember watching him walk down the road one dark night — an upright, strutting walk — and thinking he looked like a detached piece of wall. The rot started, I suppose, when he got the part of Bottom — for which, I admit, he was well suited — in his school's production of *A Midsummer Night's Dream* and he more or less ran away with the show. 'I never knew Shakespeare could be so good,' Dora said.

From there he went on to Restoration comedy and when he left school he got a job with a provincial repertory company. I don't know what sort of job it was or what parts he played, but I had to send him ten pounds a week to save him from starvation. Two years later he was in Hollywood, not, as Dora claimed, as a film star, but as a television actor and we, in fact, saw him from time to time in various cops and robbers sagas (he was invariably among the robbers) and westerns. Dora and I were often introduced, when we went out on an evening (which wasn't all that often) as Nigel's parents. He must have been rather good to have got even the minor parts and was presumably doing quite well, for although he hardly ever wrote, he phoned us every two or three months from California. The calls were never particularly satisfactory, for the thought that everything you say is costing four or five shillings a word can put a damper on almost any conversation. In any case he never told us much, for he usually phoned to ask how we were, though in the course of one conversation he mentioned — almost by the way — that he was married 'to the most beautiful girl you ever saw', and before Dora could stop pining over the fact that we had never even been invited to the wedding, he mentioned, in the course of another, that he was divorced: 'Why did I divorce her? Because she was just one hell of a bitch.' We had thought, especially since my retirement, of paying him a visit, but he never actually asked us to come,

and in any case we were a little afraid of what we might
find. We in fact never talked much about Nigel. He wasn't a
source of sorrow or disgrace, but neither was he a source of
joy.

I looked at my watch. I still had three hours to kill and I
travelled back into town with the thought of going to the
pictures, but when I got to Piccadilly I recoiled. The
commotion, the jostling, the noise, the glaring neons and
the crusted dirt, the shoddy goods, the shabby people, the
rancid smells, the tatty squalor! I suddenly felt as if I had
fallen out of my world into some seedy underworld and
experienced a yearning to be back on the coast with the
sound of the sea and the feel of the spray and the clean moist
air. I took a taxi to Victoria and did not breathe easily again
until the train was out of the station.

# 11

When I got home the phone was ringing. It was Gypsy.

'Where were you? I expected you here at eight.'

'I phoned from Victoria. Didn't you get my message?'

'It's a waste of time leaving messages, they don't understand English. Look, you had better come back into town.
Mother's been taken ill.'

'How? When? Is it serious?'

'I wouldn't have phoned you if it wasn't. Are you coming
by train?'

'No, the last train's gone. I'll drive.'

'Be careful, it's wet.'

The streets were empty so I could drive fast and I had
never driven so fast in my life, even during my youthful MG
roadster days. The needle touched a hundred for much of
the journey and sometimes exceeded it. Dora would have
had heart failure, but I found it exhilarating, even comforting. I had discovered an anodyne for worry—speed.

I had come to the car half-paralysed with apprehension. I
was nervous of pressing Gypsy for details, but I already
feared the worst, yet when I began to pick up speed, my
fears began to fade and once I went beyond eighty, they
vanished altogether, though they began to fade back in
whenever I slowed down for the lights. I got to Gypsy in an
hour and a half instead of the two and a half hours I
normally took.

Nathan came to the door. Dora must have been very
seriously ill to make *him* lose sleep. Gypsy was in the half-
darkened lounge drinking tea with two figures whom I at
first barely recognised as Arthur and Phyllis. They had only
just arrived from Manchester. Phyllis was in tears.

Nathan took my coat and offered me a whisky.

A thousand questions rushed through my mind but I
didn't know what to ask first and they didn't seem disposed
to tell me anything, or rather, they seemed to take it for
granted that I knew everything.

'Where is Dora?' I asked and they all turned to me as if I
was asking a silly question.

'St Mark's,' said Nathan. 'They had to operate.'

'*Operate?*'

'Well as you know she was—'

'He doesn't know anything,' Gypsy interjected, 'she didn't
want him to know.'

'Then perhaps someone will tell me now.'

'Mother was having treatment for a tumour.'

'That was over a year ago, it was benign, she had it out.'

'It wasn't benign, and she didn't have it out, or at least
not all of it. She had to come back for further treatment.
That's why she was in London last week and that's why she

was there again today and she had a haemorrhage. Luckily she was in hospital when it happened. They rushed her to the operating theatre there and then.'

'When?'

'About three. I was with her at the time. She may pull through, but they don't rate her chances highly.'

'They don't rate her chances at all,' said Arthur. He was a tall man with large glasses, a bushy moustache and large teeth which were always half-bared in a sort of snarl.

'Did you see her after the operation?' I asked.

'I did, but of course she was unconscious. She still is. They'll phone us when she comes round.'

'If she comes round,' said Arthur.

'Does Nigel know?'

'I phoned him,' said Nathan, 'he'll be here in the morning.' I was rather touched and reassured by his solicitude. He poured me another whisky. Phyllis was sobbing bitterly.

'Why don't you come upstairs and lie down?' said Gypsy. 'Come on, let me take you.'

She shook her head.

'Why didn't she tell me?'

Gypsy put an arm round her.

'That's Mother. She didn't like worrying people. She wouldn't have told me either if I hadn't got it out of her. She'll be all right.'

'Why didn't you phone me when she was here last week, you knew then?'

'I only knew she was getting treatment, I didn't know how serious it was.'

'It was only cancer,' said Arthur.

'I spoke to her yesterday,' sobbed Phyllis. 'She gave no hint, no hint. She said she was fine and was looking forward to having us all down at Easter.'

'Look, there's no point in upsetting yourself. Let me take you upstairs, you've had a tiring journey.'

'It was I who had the tiring journey,' said Arthur. 'Didn't

take my foot off the accelerator till I came up your drive. It's
no fun driving two hundred miles along wet roads with
someone sobbing at your side all the way. She couldn't have
been taken ill at a more awkward moment.'

'No doubt Mrs Newman will apologise when she gets
better,' said Nathan drily.

There was silence again.

It began to rain, lightly at first, then heavily. The
windows rattled with the weight of the downpour.

'It'll be murder getting back,' said Arthur. 'The roads'll
be flooded. And I've got to get back. There's a meeting of
the University Court at five.'

'Perhaps you'd like to go now,' said Gypsy.

Phyllis broke down again and he turned upon her with
impatience.

'Have you taken your valium? I presume you haven't. She
has a whole medicine cupboard crammed full of potions
and pills which she never takes, or takes in the wrong
order—not that it would matter if she took them in the right
order, for they cancel each other out—librium, valium,
lithium, barium, schmarium, aquarium. You name them,
she's got them. It's not a house we're running, it's a bloody
pharmacy. And it's not as if she gets them on the National
Health. You've no idea—'

'Arthur,' said Gypsy sweetly, 'the river's just at the back of
the house.'

'What about it?'

'Why don't you go and jump in?'

The phone rang. We all froze. It was Nigel speaking from
New York. He was between planes and expected to reach
London before breakfast. Nathan arranged to pick him up
at the airport.

'Will you recognise him?' said Gypsy.

'He's seen him often enough on television,' said Arthur.

'But he won't be wearing a bandalero across his chest or a
sombrero on his head.'

I wondered if I would recognise him. I hadn't seen him

for fifteen years. I felt apprehensive at the thought of meeting him, or perhaps I was merely transferring the apprehensions I felt about Dora. I was so full of conflicting emotions I wasn't sure what I felt. They didn't quite amount to pain, the sharp stab of agony I felt when David had his heart attack. Of course he had been much younger, unmarried, unrealised, without children. He had started out with so much promise and had achieved nothing, which was tragic in itself, but perhaps the sort of bond one had between a husband and wife could never amount to the sort one had between brothers. Or perhaps I was just calmed by optimism. She was a tough old bird, and not that old either. She would pull through. Yet I somehow didn't feel entitled to be as composed as I was, without any sense of contrition. The moment she collapsed was probably the moment I was in that hotel bedroom with Iris, which was perhaps why I couldn't rise to the occasion. There was a strange telepathy between Dora and me, and there is, I suppose, between most husbands and wives after about ten years of marriage. We spoke in half sentences, which was partly because nobody had much of a chance of finishing a sentence when Dora was around, but partly because she nearly always knew what was in my mind. I say nearly, because if she had known everything, our marriage wouldn't have lasted.

She had been taken seriously ill once before, while I was at work, and I had a strange premonition that all was not well. Minutes later the phone went.

I had had a similar premonition earlier this evening, all the way home in the train, the feeling that something unfortunate had happened, or was about to happen, only I did not connect it with Dora and thought that it had something to do with my unfortunate experience early in the afternoon. By the time I got home it was so overwhelming that I couldn't face being in the house alone and I got the car out and drove over to Ada's. Happily she was in. 'Long time no see,' she said and threw her arms round me and my foreboding vanished almost at once and it seemed to me that all it had amounted to was a fear that, to use Mrs Telfer's expression, my equipment was not in working order. The few hours with Ada had assured me that it was. It was thus nearly midnight before Gypsy could get hold of me. I should have had some feeling of guilt, but I had none. Perhaps I was too weary and numb to feel anything: perhaps I had a subconscious belief that I was entitled to Ada and that after nearly forty years of married life a man is entitled to a mistress as a long-service employee is entitled to a gold watch. In fact my mind was so full of Ada that I found it difficult to focus my concern on Dora and I wondered whether I should go and see her.

'At this time of the night?' said Nathan.

'They allow you in at any time in emergencies.'

'They'd let you see her,' said Gypsy, 'but she's not in a condition to see you. You'd do nothing for her and only upset yourself.'

'And you'd be in the way,' said Nathan.

'Is she in a coma?'

'She hasn't come out of the anaesthetic and she's all tangled up with bottles and tubes, not a pleasant sight.'

'I feel so helpless sitting here.'

'You wouldn't be any less helpless sitting there and infinitely less comfortable.'

'It might be his last chance to see the old girl,' said Arthur. 'Why not pop in for a quick squint? I'll drive you round.'

'If she caught sight of you she'd have a relapse,' said Gypsy. 'I've spoken to the surgeon and there is no point in any of us going there at this moment. She mustn't be disturbed and it wouldn't do us much harm to get some sleep ourselves. There are enough beds in the place. Father, do lie down.'

'I'm all right where I am.'

'I might as well get some sleep,' said Arthur rising and then, almost as an afterthought, he turned to Phyllis. 'Aren't you coming?'

She shook her head, the tears flying from her face like spray.

'Please yourself. See you in the morning.'

I didn't want to move but I must have fallen asleep and when I woke it was daylight. I found a travel rug round me and a familiar voice in an unfamiliar accent was coming from the kitchen next door. It was Nigel. He greeted me with a loud 'Hi, how you doing, Dad?' and a punch on the shoulder which sent me reeling. 'Well, what do you think? She's pulled through, hasn't she? I knew she would.'

'When did you hear?'

'Now. They rang a minute ago. Jesus, women like Mum don't die, they have to be put down.'

He was as broad as ever but had filled out a bit in front and looked like Dora at her most robust. He sounded a bit like her too. I gave him a punch on the shoulder and he punched me back.

'What's this?' asked Nathan, 'A family reunion or a sparring match?' And Nigel punched him too.

'Don't start with Nathan,' warned Gypsy, 'he boxed for the navy.'

'Who against,' said Nigel, 'the Wrens?'

Two days passed before Dora was allowed visitors and I got a shock when I saw her. She was, as Gypsy said, all tangled up with bottles and tubes and lay back on her pillow, a white-faced, white-haired, frail, wasted, crumpled little creature, trying vainly to smile and unable to utter a word. She nodded her head slightly, as if to say, 'I'll be all right.' A pang shot through me and I wasn't sure if it was affection or pride. Perhaps it was both.

By the end of the week she was able to sit up and talk, though in a voice which wasn't quite hers. I held her hand and it didn't have its familiar, taut, padded feel. The skin was loose on the bones, like an over-large glove.

'You hate me, don't you?' she said.

'Hate?' I said, 'I've never hated anyone in my life.'

'I know, but you hate me and I don't blame you for hating me. I've messed up your life.'

'Messed up—three beautiful children.'

'Yes, but they've grown up and live their own lives, I mean now. You wouldn't have retired if it wasn't for me.'

'Let's not talk about that.'

'But I want to talk about it. I've had time to think. I've thought about nothing else, it was a selfish and criminal thing to do.'

'What do you mean? It would have been criminal not to have sold out when I did. Who could have said no to an offer like that?'

'Money never meant anything to you, Sidney. You don't like to spend it, but you never lived for it or worried about it.'

'What Jewish businessman doesn't worry about money?'

'You were never much of a businessman and, for that matter, not much of a Jew either. Which reminds me, Sidney, I don't want to be cremated.'

'Why the sudden talk of cremations?'

'Please Sidney, don't interrupt me. I tire easily and this is important. I don't know what there is after death, if anything, but if you burn something, that's it, no second thoughts. If you remember, I didn't even burn old newspapers, I put them out in a special box in case I should want to read them again. I don't want to be cremated and I want to be buried in one piece—and not with the Federation of Synagogues, Sidney. Father was buried with the Federation and they never looked after the graves properly. The whole cemetery was a jungle. The United Synagogue keep their cemeteries tidy. Bushey, I'd like to be buried in Bushey.' She grasped my hand tightly. 'Sidney, promise you'll bury me in Bushey.'

'Dora my love, you'll outlive us all.'

'Thanks for the comfort,' and she began crying. I had never seen her in tears before—she was the invincible member of our partnership—and it upset me. I sat there grasping her hand and feeling helpless.

'I'm sorry,' she said, 'it's not like me.'

'Everybody's entitled to cry now and again.'

'I've never cried before.'

'Then you're all the more entitled to it.'

'I'm not myself. I lost all my blood you know. They gave me gallons of somebody else's blood and I don't know who I am, or what I am. How do I look?'

'A bit pale, why?'

'They could have given me the blood of a *schwartzer*.'

'You haven't turned black if that's what you're afraid of.'

'I don't feel myself.'

'You sound yourself.'

'I've been very selfish, Sidney.'

'You, selfish?'

'Very. Why do you think I made you retire?'

'No one made me do anything I didn't want to do.'

'I knew this was coming up—I didn't think it would be coming so soon, but I could feel it and I thought it would be nice that if I had another three or four years to go, if we could make a new start, in a new house, just you and me. We've been married all these years and all our lives has been children and business, business and children and the business has really been for the children and I thought it would be nice before everything was over if we had a few years to ourselves and I thought when that offer came in, this is it, it's a sign from heaven.'

'I never knew you were that religious.'

'What woman isn't religious? And I thought if you didn't retire now you never would, but I was sorry. I was sorry when you sold out and I saw what it did to you. I was even sorrier when we moved. I haven't known many men in my life and I hadn't realised how attached they get to things. Mother said she could only get Father to emigrate when the pogromchicks burned their house down. I was your pogromchick, so why shouldn't you hate me?'

'I don't hate you. You had the sense to make me do the right thing.'

'Selling out and moving was a disaster and this is my punishment.'

'Punishment? You'll be all right. You haven't been ill before? I haven't been ill before?'

'Sidney, I know what I'm talking about. I'm a dying woman.'

'We'll have a good laugh over this conversation in another week or two.'

'You may, I won't. And listen, Sidney, don't forget what I told you, it's Bushey I want to be buried in. No cremations, no Federation — Bushey.'

'And supposing you should outlive me?'

'Heaven forbid, you're still in your prime, which brings me to my next thing. I want you to marry again, and the sooner the better. You're still of an age when you could make some woman happy. If you leave it for another year or two you'll be past it and you'll have to live with the children. We have wonderful children, Sidney, wonderful; and sometimes when I'm a little sorry for myself I ask what I did to deserve them, but to have children living with you is one thing and to live with your children is another. If you ask me, it's a punishment for living too long. You wouldn't be happy with Gypsy. She's got a wonderful house, a palace and servants, but you worship her too much to be under the same roof, you'd never have a relaxed moment. As for Phyllis, she's a darling, but — and I haven't told this to a soul — I can't stand the sight of Arthur, I don't know how she can. He may be very educated and clever, but he's stupid — '

'And pompous.'

'And pompous, but I don't even mind that, what I can't stand is when he tries to be jocular and breezy — he wasn't like that when he first married, was he?'

'No, he was just pompous and stupid, but I think he's been trying to cultivate a sense of humour.'

'And the thing with these University professors is they have such long holidays. He's always at home. You wouldn't be able to stand it. And as for Nigel, I don't even know if he's married and if he is he could be married to a man for

87

all I know, he's an actor after all and living in California and you've no idea the crazy things they get up to out there. No, Sidney, you've got to marry. Women can always manage on their own, but men are helpless. I remember my own poor father. You'll have to marry and soon and I've got the very woman for you — Iris.'

'I —'

'Don't interrupt.'

'She —'

'I said don't interrupt. I'm a dying woman, Sidney, so if you don't mind I'd like the last word. It so happens — and I think this was from heaven too — I spoke to her on the very day I took ill and asked her why she didn't come down to see us and she promised she would. She's made for you more than I was. If you ask me I probably wasn't made for you. Your mother said I wasn't and she may have been right. Mothers know. I know, I'm a mother. Now what was I saying? Yes, Iris. She may play a bit hard to get, but believe me, she'll have you like a shot. I know she's not Jewish and your mother wouldn't have been happy about it, but as I said you're not much of a Jew — you won't forget Sidney, no cremation —'

'I won't forget.'

'As I said, you're not much of a Jew, if anything Iris is more Jewish than you are and perhaps she'll make a bit of a Jew out of you. You could start in business again. You may feel a bit old for it, but she's not fifty and a very bright piece of goods and she'll have you like a shot. I don't know if I should be telling you this, in fact I shouldn't be telling you this, but I'll tell it to you all the same. You know there was something between her and your brother David.'

'Who told you?'

'Nobody tells me anything, but I know everything. I tell you there was, and I think she was half-way to becoming Jewish when he died. Did I tell you I once found a Jewish prayer book in her desk? No, I didn't tell you, but I did, a Jewish prayer book in her desk.'

'What were you doing in her desk?'

'I was looking for something in your desk.'

'But you said it was in *her* desk.'

'Your desk, her desk, what does it matter? And seeing she couldn't get David first-hand, she'll take you second-hand, but don't leave it too long. She won't wait forever. A month after the funeral will be long enough. And Sidney?'

'Yes.'

'Remember, no cremation.'

Her voice, instead of fading, swelled as she continued and by the end of the week she was able to get out of bed and walk a little round the ward, though leaning heavily on my arm. A week later Gypsy was able to bring her home for convalescence. Nigel met her at the door and lifted her up in both arms as if she was a doll. Gypsy screamed with alarm.

'You idiot. She'll come undone.'

'Not my mom,' said Nigel, 'she's made out of steel.' She had filled out slightly and there was even a bit of colour in her cheek.

The doctor had ordered that she stay in bed, but she insisted on sitting up in a chair.

'I hate the sight of ceilings,' she said.

'But the doctor said—'

'The doctor can go to hell. It's funny how people believe in nothing else these days but when a doctor speaks they think it comes from heaven. What do doctors know?'

'That's unkind, mother,' said Gypsy, 'they saved your life.'

'Saved my life? They nearly killed me in the first place. If somebody pushed you into the river and then dives in to pull you out, do you have to feel grateful to him?'

I was reassured by the sound of her even more than the sight of her.

'You seem much better,' I said.

'Better,' she said, 'but not so much better that I'll live for ever—so don't forget Bushey.'

'Bushey?' said Nigel, 'Bushey? Are you going to move?'
'He's not,' said Dora, 'I am.'

# 12

I had spent so much of my time coming and going from
hospital that I had hardly had a chance to speak to Nigel
and he, for his part, seemed to have spent much of his time
with different theatrical agents, trying to tie up some sort of
deal, though I suspected that whatever it was hadn't come
off, for he looked a little crestfallen. He arranged to fly back
to America the day after Dora left hospital and I drove him
to Heathrow and it was only then that he told me he had
married again, a young divorcée with two children.

'You should see her, Dad, the most beautiful girl in the
world, a bit like Gypsy, but more zing.'

'More what?'

'Zing.'

'What's zing?'

'It's difficult to describe, but you know it when you see it
and I want you to see it. As soon as Mum is well enough to
travel, I want you two to come out there—even if I have to
come and get you.'

'You could have told us you'd remarried.'

'I could have, I should have, but, hell, you know how it is.
These things take time to take. I wanted to be sure it was the
real thing before I said anything about it.'

'Are you sure it's the real thing now?'

'It couldn't be realer.'

'You've got no children of your own yet?'

'You mean a joint effort? No, not yet, but give us time. We've only been married two years.'

'How long does it take to have a child in America?'

'They're an expensive commodity, kids, especially in California, about the most expensive thing going, and the older they get the more expensive they become.'

'Look, if you can't afford to raise a family, I can still help out with a quid or two.'

'Dad, have I ever asked you for help?'

'No, well not recently.'

'It's nothing to do with money, but Jo's not Phyllis you know—'

'There's nothing wrong with Phyllis.'

'Did I say there was?'

'No but, suddenly, being a mother—and a good mother at that—has become a crime against society.'

'Hell, Jo's a marvellous mother, you should see her kids— they could have walked out of a TV commercial—but she's got talent, a career. She's a graphic designer, earns more than I do and earns it regularly. She's working, I'm working and somehow we haven't been able to fit a kid into our schedule.'

'If I had worked on that principle I don't know if I could have fitted you into my schedule.'

'I sometimes wish you hadn't.'

'Are things that bad?'

'They've been worse, but then I was younger and when you're young no matter how lousy things are, you can still dream of your big break. I'm almost past the age of dreaming.'

'You're in your mid-thirties.'

'That's nearly past the age of dreaming. This is crisis point. Nearly forty and not yet a top name—and there isn't much use for bottom names in this game. What's on my side is that I don't play romantic leads, but even character parts have a limited age range. The younger fellows can play older ones, but not always the other way about, and I still haven't had my big break — they don't write big parts for my sorts of talents. So until the big break comes I've got to take anything going, walk-on parts, walk-off parts, bit-parts, shit-parts, films, the box, commercials, anything to keep the name in circulation, not only in the directories, but before the public and if you're not in big lights already, you've got to keep flickering for all you're worth. There's guys who rough up their wives, their sisters, their mothers even, just to keep their names moving. If it's in the newspapers in the morning and on the box at night, it'll be everywhere the day after. I half-killed my first wife. You've never met her, have you? You'd have hated her. I found her in bed with this chico and beat the living daylights out of her, him too. Not for publicity you understand, she had it coming. I don't think I left her with two whole bones in her body, but she crawled to the neighbours, they drove her to her mother and that was the end of that. It might never have happened. Something like that could be worth a million dollars in publicity.'

I nearly went off the road as he continued with his chronicle.

'Isn't there such a thing as bad publicity?' I asked.

'Not in show business. The only bad publicity is no publicity.'

'Did you have any children?' (an odd question, it struck me, for a father to ask of his son, but he was an odd son).

'Children? With that whore? Hell no, I'm about the only one who hasn't. But you don't think about anything else, do you, it's kids, kids or nothing. I used to think you weren't like that. You didn't pull me into your business, like other Jewish dads, or push me into the professions, but you're just like the rest of them, no life of your own but just living for kids and kids' kids. You're not doing too badly. Phyllis has got four — I hope to hell they don't take after their father — and Gypsy's still in her twenties.'

'She's thirty.'

'Hell, there's women of fifty who have kids.'
'She won't have any children.'
'What makes you so sure?'
'I'm sure.'
'How well do you know Gypsy?'
'Enough to know that she won't be having children.'
'You've spoken to her gynaecologist?'
'I've spoken to Gypsy.'
'And what did she tell you, her fallopians are snarled up?'
'I don't have to go into details.'
'You've forgotten what she was like as a kid, so full of fantasies that she didn't know when she was telling the truth and when she wasn't.'
'That was a very long time ago.'
'Did she tell you that Nathan was a pouf?'
'A what?'
'A faggot, a fruit, a fairy, a pansy, a nancy, a bum-boy, a pederast, a queer, a homosexual, a sodomite, a bugger.'
'I've caught your meaning. Did she tell you he was?'
'She didn't, but Mother almost hinted that he might be,' and he broke into a loud cackle, like the sound of eggs being beaten (in the pre-Kenwood days). 'From the sort of questions she asked me she was half afraid that I was.'
'I think that's your mother's way of showing she knows what's going on in the world, though to be honest I don't know what's going on in the world myself.'
'Nathan's no pouf.'
'What makes you so sure? I'm not saying he is, but what makes you so sure he's not?'
'I'm an actor. I've lived among them and worked among them all my life. They send out signals like a skunk sends out smells. He may not be interested in sex, but that doesn't make him a pouf and in any case I'm not sure if sex means all that much to Gypsy. Her one true love is herself, if you ask me and she doesn't like sharing. Two's a crowd as far as she's concerned. I'm not saying she's sexless. All I'm saying is she's not smouldering with it. It's not that important.'

'What isn't?'

'Sex.'

'That's a strange thought coming from an American.'

'You get people who are colour-blind, or tone-deaf, or deaf to religion and it's the same with sex. You can do without it — take the Pope. I'm not saying Gypsy's that way, but what I am saying is that it's no great tragedy if she is. It's not as if she's at home kicking her heels. She's a bright kid, I wish I was half as good an actor as she is a lawyer— my name would be up there in lights. She's my lawyer, you know.'

'Why do you need a lawyer in London if you're living in Los Angeles?'

'Acting is a multi-national occupation. I've got a lawyer in Rome too, a lousy one, I'm suing the bastard. Gypsy's tying something up for me now, only I've got to rush back for some stinking commercials. Also Jo doesn't like to be left long on her own with the kids. She gets nervy. Los Angeles isn't London. You know a fellow in my sort of occupation, always on the go, can do with a wife-sitter, only you can't trust anyone with your wife unless you took their balls off and what use would they be if you did? I'm not saying I wouldn't trust Jo—I'm talking in general.'

'Why not try hiring a what-did-you call them?'

'A pouf? They're the worst of the lot. They're not eunuchs, you know. They're game for any opening, a hole in the ground if they can find nothing else. The little chico I caught with my first wife was a dinky little fairy. What she needed was a chastity belt. Jo's not like that but she's nervy on her own. It's natural if you've got two small kids.'

'How old are they?'

'How old? Four, I think, and maybe nine. I know what you're thinking, it's about time we added one of ours to the score.'

'I didn't say a thing.'

'It's what you said before. Well, we will. I've got a year or two to go yet before my change in life. If this break comes I'll do nothing else. I'll take a year off and breed.'

'I don't know what they teach you about these things in America, but it doesn't take a year.'

'Yes, but I've got to make up for lost time. I'll have kids, lots of them. Phyllis'll have more. Gypsy too, maybe. You'll be overwhelmed with kids and the name of Newman shall ring forth unto the end of time — but in the meantime, can I ask a favour? Smile a little. I haven't seen your face crack once in the three weeks I've been here.'

'You haven't come at a smiling time.'

'I don't remember you smiling much at any time.'

'Maybe you didn't bring out the smiles in me.'

'Oh Christ, you still can't forgive me for not going into the business, can you?'

'You dismissed my company as a twopenny-halfpenny affair —'

'That still rankles.'

'It wouldn't if you had achieved anything better, but you said yourself that you should be at the peak of your career and you're nowhere.'

'I'm not nowhere, Christ, I'm Nigel Newman. Wait till you come out to L.A. People stop me in the streets, kids clamour for my autograph. I show my face in a restaurant and I'm led to the best table. Cops stop traffic to let me cross. But I still haven't had my big break. It'll come. I've been seeing people in London and New York, tying up odds and ends. In show business you never count a deal as done until you've got the money and spent it. If I was religious I'd offer up a prayer.'

'You should have asked your mother —'

'Is she religious?'

'She wasn't, but we all change.'

'You've got to bring her out to L.A., then you'll see what I am. It'll do her good.'

'Nigel, your mother's past travelling.'

'I don't mean this week or next, but in a few months. She's a gutsy old bird. If she survived that crisis she'll outlive us all. It was the same with Grandma, remember? The women are sick and the men drop dead. You've got nothing to worry about. If you'll be up to it, she will.'

As we came into the terminal I was startled by the sound of his name being called loudly and urgently over the loud-speakers.

'I'll look after your luggage,' I said quickly, 'you go to the enquiry desk,' but he seemed to be in no hurry.

'Is this something you arranged to keep your name in circulation?'

'Every little helps. Look around you, the place is milling with people. Important people some of them.'

'They're mostly Arabs.'

'Nobody's more important than an Arab these days and when they hear the name again it'll ring a bell and that's what this is all about — to keep the bells ringing.'

But I was troubled by the urgency in the announcer's voice. She kept repeating his name every few seconds.

'Aren't you going to answer the call?'

'In a minute. Listen to her, a good clear voice. There's a bit of drama building up. People are beginning to stop and look up. You can see it in their faces. "Who is this Nigel Newman? Can he be *the* Nigel Newman? Why are they calling him? What's happened?"'

'Look,' I said, 'it's getting on my nerves. If you don't answer the call, I will.'

He put a calming hand on my shoulder. 'Steady old boy, where's your British phlegm? 'I arranged it all with a friend,' he explained.

'That's obvious, but if after twenty years on the stage you still need to go in for that sort of thing, then perhaps you should do something else for a living.'

'A living? No one in his senses turns to the stage for a living. I'm hooked, don't you understand? Mom was telling me she could never forgive herself for making you retire, because your business was your life — well, the stage is mine.'

'Business may have been my life, but at least it gave me a livelihood—'

Our conversation, which was getting a little heated, was cut short by a further call on the loudspeaker for Nigel Newman.

'The bum's overdoing it,' he said impatiently and hurried over to enquiry desk. He returned a moment later white-faced, shaken. 'It's Mom, she's had a relapse.'

PART II

*A Newer Life*

# 1

I found several letters waiting for me when I arrived, presumably condolence letters. I don't know who ever thought up condolence letters, for they don't console. It is, I suppose, good to know that there are people who share your grief, but it's difficult to put sincere grief into words without sounding insincere and what you get is formulae and fulsomeness and overfulsomeness. When Mother died I had people ransacking the dictionaries for qualities they could put to her name — generous, understanding, warm-hearted, compassionate, wise. She was none of these things, but a peevish little woman who cared a lot for her children and nothing for anyone else.

I wasn't even all that grief-stricken when she died. She had lived to be eighty-eight and towards the end of her life she had become impossible to herself and to everybody else, especially poor Dora, and when she passed away it was only Michaelson who had the honesty and insight to say to me: 'Well, I'll bet you're glad that's over,' which was perhaps an exaggeration, but not all that far from the truth.

I was inconsolable when David died, but then I couldn't face the great pile of condolence letters which rained down on me and left them unopened for two or three months and then it was like an opening of wounds.

On this occasion I opened the letters after only a slight hesitation and the first, I was relieved to see, was from Michaelson:


Dear Sid,

I don't much like writing condolence letters and like receiving them even less, so you needn't worry, this is not a letter of condolence. Dora — at least until her last few

101

months—lived a good, full and healthy life and nobody should want to live much beyond seventy. I am over seventy myself and it's a favour I could do without.

But why the hell didn't you let me know? You were so secretive about the whole thing I thought that maybe you had killed the old girl and had run for it to America. Ironic, though isn't it, your fine, plump, healthy, robust Dora dying and my frail little wraith still fluttering on. She'll be the death of me yet.

But to turn to a more cheerful subject, or at least to the one subject which can still cheer me up. I have discovered some new friends and in particular a woman of mature years, as they say, and with mature endowments and what is more who is anxious to share them. Her husband is something or other for someone or other and is away most of the time and even when he's at home he's unable, or unwilling, to satisfy her in the manner to which she would like to become accustomed. And where do you think she lives? Over the road from you. In fact I was knocking on your door and she happened to pass by, we got into conversation and one thing led to another and this other, I tell you, is like some place I've never been before. It's like walking down a perfectly familiar street, past houses and shops you've seen before and people you've met before and finding yourself suddenly in paradise. A fine, healthy piece of goods with red cheeks, bright eyes and as firm as a football (which maybe has been kicked about a bit) and she's ready for it any time of the day or night, even, would you believe it, after breakfast! She also prefers the more mature male (I doubt if it's what she prefers, but it's what she gets for I was passing her house the other day and saw a fellow in a wheelchair coming out—though maybe he wasn't in a wheelchair going in). And the things she can get up to (or down to) and make you get up to! You've heard of the old saying that you can't teach an old dog new tricks, well she can.

So you see you don't know what's under your own nose till you're no longer there to enjoy it. If you'll find anything as good in America (which I doubt, for they're very tall, American women, and their vigour is spread over too big an area) good luck to you, but if not, believe me it's worth coming back here, if only on a visit.

M

I found it difficult to make out the signature of the next letter, but I recognised the writer from his very first sentence.

Dear Mr Newman,

I was sorry to hear the missus had passed on. I only heard about it by chance as I no longer work at Scandawools as they've had a reorganisation and I've been reorganised out of my job. I'd have come to the funeral, only it was all over by the time I'd heard about it. I was at the wedding, if you remember, in Hackney Synagogue and she was the prettiest bride since Queen Mary (or Princess Mary of Teck as she then was) at whose wedding I also had the privilege of being present (though I wasn't invited, as in the case of your wedding, but was on the pavement outside). She was the life and soul of our Christmas parties (the missus I mean, not Princess Mary of Teck) and did the liveliest Knees-up-Mother-Brown I ever saw and she did me many a favour, like visiting my mother when she was down, with whatever it was she was down with (I don't think they ever found out and my neighbour thought I'd poisoned her, though if there was one person I should have poisoned it was my neigh-bour — she's still alive, so it was a pity I didn't) and laid her out when she was dead and came to the funeral as well. So did you, of course, but she had one of the nippers on the way (I think it was Miss Phyllis) and by the look of her she was ready to have it there and then. And she always remem-bered my birthday even though I didn't (though I should have done, for I was born on the same day as the Queen Mother).

103

I am enjoying my retirement more than I thought I would (though of course I miss the company). I do a good bit of fishing (though I don't catch many fish—I don't think there's that many left to catch) and I'm experimenting with growing tea in my allotment, the price of tea being shocking (they say coffee is worse). If it goes on at this rate we'll all have to turn to drink—I still haven't touched the whisky the missus gave me as a retiring present, as I didn't feel entitled to it because I didn't really retire. I suppose I'm entitled to it now, but I'm saving it for a rainy day. I still get around on me own steam, which is more than most people do at my age (especially as most people are dead at my age) and being a member of the Church sick visiting committee, I still do a bit of hospital visiting, especially round the day wards to cheer people up. You'll remember the comedy turns I used to do at the Christmas party—especially the impersonation of Lloyd George and Stanley Baldwin—well they still go down well and I suppose when you're propped up in bed or a chair, not been able to do much, a laugh's about the best thing for you. The nurses enjoy it too and in fact they begin to giggle before I even start. Matron thinks I should turn professional, but it's a bit late for that now.

I saw Master Nigel on television the other night. He was on a horse at the time and riding fast and he was hardly on the screen before he was off, but I recognised him right away, even though he had a moustache running from one end of his face to the other. I remember him helping out in the warehouse during the summer holidays and him telling me he was hoping to go on the stage. Well everybody does, don't they? Little did I think that in another few years he'd be famous. She must have been proud of him, your missus. I'll miss her.

Yours,<br>Leslie.

The next letter was from Iris, as I feared it would be.

Dearest Sidney,

(The 'dearest' may sound presumptuous, but 'dear' would have been a little peremptory). This will probably be one of those letters which I wish I hadn't sent (I may be very clear-headed in business, but I'm a bit muddled when it comes to my own life—isn't everybody?).

I'm upset and as you will see, I think I have a right to be (or is it that I have worked so long among Jews that I have acquired a touch of Jewish paranoia?) though I am perhaps more upset with myself than anybody else. I keep remembering the unforgiveable questions I asked you at lunch and the unforgiveable things I said the very day, perhaps even the very hour poor Dora collapsed, but will you believe me when I say I had no idea she was dying of cancer? As you know, I spoke to her some minutes before I met you and she gave no hint of her illness. Neither did anyone else and if you knew anything about it, you said nothing (nor frankly, did you behave as if you knew anything). And knowing nothing of that I, of course, knew nothing of her operation, her relapse and her tragic death and would have known nothing but for the fact that I happened to pick up an old copy of *The Times* in Helsinki (where I was on business) and read the death announcement. At first I thought it couldn't be the same Newman, not only because it was unlike Dora to die, but because I felt that surely someone would have told me, but just to make sure I phoned your home and when I got no reply, I phoned Gypsy and it was she who told me everything, adding, almost as an afterthought, that you had left for America.

Don't you think I had a right to know? Couldn't you have phoned me when Dora was in hospital? I was often exasperated with her and I had to go to elaborate lengths to keep her out of sight when you entertained important customers, but I loved the woman, as did everyone who knew her—if not always at first encounter. Even your mother once told me grudgingly, 'she may be common, but she's good.' It was Dora who, more than anyone else, made me feel part of the family (perhaps she clutched at me because being 'common', she felt a bit of an outsider herself). If it wasn't for her I'd probably have left Scandawools years ago. Oh, I was fond of you and I liked the people, but I could have earned nearly twice as much elsewhere. (I'm earning more than twice as much now—my expense allowance alone comes to more than you paid me—there, wouldn't I make a splendid shidduch for someone, especially if he should not only be short of a wife, but a secretary?) I know I'd have got more if I asked, but it was difficult to do so when you were taking out so little yourself. I liked your whole family, even Nigel (why didn't you tell me he was here—I haven't seen him since he was a child). I love Gypsy and experienced something like family pride in watching her grow into the exquisite creature she is, but in a way Dora meant more to me than anyone. There was her openness and spontaneity and—very unJewish this—her inability to take slights. She wasn't thick-skinned—as your mother thought. On the contrary, in some ways she was the most sensitive person in your family, but she had made up her mind, possibly early in your married life, when all of the family were against her, to be above slights. Even with you I've always had to be somewhat on guard, so that even while I'm writing this I keep wondering whether I should post it—but never with Dora.

I am not unambitious. As I said I could have earned more and found jobs with better prospects, but I was trading opportunities for acceptance and I do not think—and certainly did not think while Dora was alive—myself presumptuous in regarding myself as one of the family. Now, with Dora gone, I am not so sure. I was aware that with your retirement and the take-over, things could not quite continue along the old lines, but I naturally took it for granted that we would keep in touch and in fact I had half planned to spend a week or two with you in the summer, but it seems as if the moment poor Dora took ill you decided to freeze me out. Phyllis who used to write to me regularly, stopped writing. Gypsy, who phoned me at least once a week, stopped phoning, and you too have kept your distance. It was as if you found sickness or death too intimate an occasion to share with a shiksa. Perhaps an outsider can never really intrude among Jews and shouldn't even try. I should have learned my lesson with poor David. But are you so afraid of me that you had to run without a word of greeting? Am I suffering from paranoia, or have I a right to be upset?

Iris.

The final letter was from Gypsy.


Dear Daddy,

Just a brief note of warning. Iris phoned shortly after you left and was very upset — as she had every right to be — that neither you nor I had told her anything. She asked for your address and will no doubt be writing to you, but before she does, will you write her a nice, sweet letter explaining — as I did — that you were thrown into a tizzy by mother's death and you weren't quite sure what you were doing. I am very fond of Iris, but would hate to have her as an enemy.

Love,<br>Gypsy.

'Dearest Iris,' I began and got no further. If I had written 'Dear' she would have been offended, but Dearest was an expression which I hadn't used even when writing to Dora. Such expressions as Dearest or Darling never had currency in our household, but I wasn't even sure that I wanted to enter into correspondence at all. I felt very close to Iris and grateful to her, but possibly because I was grateful and close, maintaining contact with her was something of an undertaking. I had been sorry to retire and start 'a new life'

107

as Dora called it, but—and this was something which I had been slow to confess even to myself—it came with a slight feeling of relief, not because it meant an end to business worries, for certain worries become almost like friends if you live with them long enough, but because it meant an escape from Iris. With Iris in the office and Dora in the home it was like having two wives. Dora was openly domineering, Iris was subtly domineering. It was always 'Don't you think?' or 'Wouldn't you prefer to?', or, 'Wouldn't you say?' but whatever I thought or preferred or said, more often than not she got her way, as did Dora, but Dora got her way because I was too weary to argue and Iris got hers because more often than not she was right and in fact the odd occasions that she turned out to be wrong (though never disastrously wrong) I had a small holiday in my heart.

I also felt troubled about that unfortunate incident on the carpet and in the hotel in a way that I hadn't been troubled by my affairs with Ada, or, what was her name, Mrs Telfer, or Shirley, because I suppose they gave her yet another claim on me. She had so many already. There was all she had done for Scandawools, there was the wasted years and shattered hopes with David, and then, finally, that. It wasn't as if I had seduced her in the first blush of maidenhood, in fact if anyone had been seduced, it was me, but it left me feeling that I should make an honest woman out of her, to do for her what poor David had left undone. Perhaps she felt the same, which is probably why I jumped so readily on Nigel's suggestion that I should go back with him to California, so that her last line wasn't all that far from the truth. I wondered if there was any point in writing at all, for she was far too intelligent to be fobbed off with excuses, yet I had to say something and I wrote along the lines suggested by Gypsy, adding: 'I don't know how long I'll be here, for I feel far too old for yet another new life and I am already beginning to miss England and the south coast and in any case I can't see what I'll do with myself. I expect to be back in another few weeks, but if not perhaps you could come out here for a bit?'

It seemed a fairly safe invitation to make from a distance of six thousand miles.

# 2

Nigel's wife, Jo, came to meet me at the airport. She wasn't in the least like Gypsy, who is tall and stately, but a little wisp of a girl, with long hair and large eyes. She looked like a child herself and it was difficult to believe that she could be the mother of two children. She shot out from among the crowd and flung herself upon me with such force that at first I wasn't quite sure what hit me. 'I've heard so much about you,' she said, which always makes me feel slightly nervous. 'You're going to love it here.' I found the warmth and sunshine a little comforting. It had been cold, wet and blustery in London. Here the temperature must have been about eighty. We drove in an open car with Jo giving a running commentary on the passing scene. It was difficult to follow what she was saying for she drove at speed, along flyovers and underpasses, through cuttings and over bridges, with great roaring torrents of cars on every side. 'You'll have to get used to this,' she said, 'these gas guzzlers are choking the country and poisoning the environment,' but I found it an exhilarating sight, like fast-flowing, colourful rivers. There was no thrombosis of cars like you find at the end of every fast road in England, but everything flowed on and on, at great speed.

'Tell me if I'm going too fast for you,' she said.

'You can't go too fast for me.'

'Mother's hair curls if I do over forty.'
'No, I love speed.'
'I'm doing seventy.'
'Do a hundred.'
And she did.
'Don't tell Nigel,' she shouted, 'he'll kill me if he finds out.'

It was only when she slowed down as she approached her house that a heavy, almost suffocating feeling settled upon me. It was in fact rather a nice house and was considerably bigger inside than it seemed outside, but all the windows were shut and the blinds were drawn and there were air-conditioners whining in every room.

'I know English people don't like warm rooms,' said Jo.

'But we don't live in refrigerators,' I wanted to say. I was curious to see what her children were like, but it was Sunday and Sundays they apparently spent with their father.

I had a spacious room with built-in cupboards, a studio couch, a wicker-work armchair and a television set (there were television sets in nearly all the rooms) and a bathroom complete with bath and shower next door.

'You have a bath and a nap and then we'll all have something to eat. Is there anything you would particularly like?'

'A cup of tea,' I said.

'Oh you'll have that and English tea at that—Nigel brought back a whole crate—but to eat. Do you like steak?'

'Why ask?' said Nigel. 'You make it, he'll eat it.'

I spent a long time in the bath, so long that both Nigel and Jo thumped on the door two or three times to see if I was all right. I lay there half asleep, half floating, half sinking, half hoping that I would dissolve in the suds. I had no feelings of grief or pain, but hollowness, or rather numbness. It was as if I was unable to respond to life or, for that matter, death. Gypsy and Phyllis were at first both worried as to how I might take it and when I didn't shed a tear, Phyllis, at least, was a trifle upset.

'I had always thought he loved Mummy,' she said.

Did I love her? I certainly missed her. I used to enjoy coming home to her with some titbit of news, especially good news and to discuss the day's events over supper, but that was all before I retired. There was no news to report once I retired and no events to discuss and in so far as there were, they were not discussable.

Few husbands and wives had the sort of relationship where they could be thrown into each other's company for months on end (or even weeks on end) without harm. I enjoyed coming home to Dora after a day's work, but the day's work was a necessary part of the enjoyment. When I didn't leave home in the first place I felt a prisoner and I had reacted to her, I suppose, as a prisoner might towards his jailer. Of course, had I known she was dying I would have been more understanding and less brusque, but she had engaged in an elaborate conspiracy to keep everything from me. Gypsy certainly knew. Nigel didn't and in fact there seemed to be a belief in the family that the menfolk should be shielded from the harsher realities of life. Anyway she was dead.

She was buried at the United Synagogue Cemetery in Bushey as requested with the full ceremonies and rites of the Jewish faith and several Rabbis in attendance, one of whom eulogised her at length and tried to comfort us with the thought that a woman of her piety and goodness (he had never as much as set eyes on her) would be assured of a place in the world to come. Dora may have believed in that sort of thing, I didn't, and if I had I would have found it slightly upsetting. It was, I think, Michaelson who said that the good thing about dying is that it's an end, finished, done with.

Jo prepared me a steak about three inches high which squirted blood when I cut it and I had no appetite for it even had my jaws been able to cope with it.

'He doesn't know what real steak is,' said Nigel. 'In England they eat cat's meat.'

'I always lose my appetite after a long journey,' I said.

'You've never been on a long journey,' said Nigel.

'Are you all right?' asked Jo anxiously.

'I'm fine.'

'You don't look too good. Want to see an analyst?'

'A what?'

'A psychoanalyst. I know someone only two blocks away who specialises in bereavement. When Pa died, Ma just didn't want to live. She wanted to stay in bed and die and we persuaded her to see an analyst. It wasn't quick work, nothing ever happens quickly with my poor Ma, but she got over it and she married again.'

'And divorced,' put in Nigel. 'She's now seeing an analyst who specialises in divorces. Look, don't let her rush you into anything, least of all an analyst, because you'll be out of pocket and out of your mind long before you're finished. If you don't want your steak, I'll eat it. What do you want, baked beans on toast?'

I could see Jo was hurt by his tone and I was upset to be a source of friction. I suddenly felt a pang of longing for England, which cheered me up a little, for it raised me out of my numbness. Where there's longing, there's life.

Jo said to me later, while Nigel was watching television, 'Is he always like that, so negative, I mean? He's so negative to everything.'

'You mustn't mind him,' I said, 'he's got a harsh way of putting things.'

'He's got a harsh way of doing things,' she said.

I woke early the next day, pulled the blind and the sun came streaming in, a broad, golden shaft and I sat down in the armchair wondering what I would do with myself, not only for the rest of the day, but the rest of my life.

'You'll have a whole new world on your doorstep,' said Nigel, but I didn't feel like facing a new world or, for that matter, the old one. I didn't feel in the least suicidal, but it would have been nice if my life had stopped there and then.

It was a beautiful room and looked out on cropped lawns and palm trees and white-walled villas. Nigel lived well for a struggling actor. The way he had described his situation I had expected to find him in a crumbling apartment in some decaying slum, but it looked as if struggling actors in America lived better than established ones in England. Never mind actors, he lived better than me. Of course Jo also worked. Graphics was an undefined country to me and for all I knew it brought in fortunes. I wished Dora was alive to see it and in particular the view. It was fit for a travel poster, the sort of scene we cheered ourselves with during the long, dark nights of an English winter. We used to spend half of January going through the travel folders, Dora and I. More often than not we ended up in Dorset or Devon, but we had also been to Spain, Greece and Israel. We particularly liked Israel and would have gone there more often, but Dora had relatives in Israel who always expected us not only to visit them, but to stay with them, which we did the first time we were there, though their pokey little flat was hardly big enough to accommodate them, let alone guests. So the second time we came on the quiet. They lived in Haifa, so we thought we might be safe in Ashkelon, which was almost the other end of the country, though we walked around nervously and furtively looking to right and left, like wanted men and even then we bumped into them before a week was out and were hauled ignominiously back to Haifa.

'You've got to admit,' said Dora, 'they're hospitable.'

'They're not hospitable,' I said, 'they want to punish us for not settling in Israel.'

Mother had warned me. 'All right, you may like Dora, but remember when you marry a Jewish girl you marry her whole family,' which is perhaps why so many Jewish boys marry non-Jewish girls.

I had little contact with Dora's family after we married, though we came together at weddings and funerals. Her mother was a massive, red-faced woman, with hair kept in place by a scarf whose ends somehow stood upright like horns. She didn't look quite like Battersea Power Station, yet every time I travelled out of Victoria and passed

Battersea Power Station, she always came to mind. She had a lot to put up with, poor woman, for her husband was an amiable but helpless character who could never make a living, though the children did quite well. When we got married you could see at a glance which side were the poor relatives and which side the rich. By the time Gypsy got married they had caught up on—if not overtaken—us and they showered her with extravagant, if tasteless, gifts which, after a decent interval, Gypsy passed on to a charity bazaar. At Dora's funeral they arrived in a great fleet of Daimlers and Jags. Strange what inconsequential thoughts come to mind at funerals. I remember standing near by the cemetery entrance and thinking there was something a little indelicate about coming to a funeral in a Jag.

There was some bitterness afterwards. Dora's family, though not particularly religious, took death religiously. Dora had died in hospital, but her brothers felt she should be brought home before the funeral. Nathan and Gypsy were not happy about the idea, so the older brother brought the body to his house and sat up beside it all night, saying psalms. Then before the funeral it is apparently the custom of immediate family to tear their clothes. A small man wielding a razor ceremonially cut the lapels of Dora's three brothers, but when he came towards me I recoiled and my children felt the same.

'You can get it invisibly repaired afterwards,' said a brother and I tried to explain that it wasn't the lapels I was worried about: I disliked the whole custom.

Finally, her family remained at home for a week of mourning, while my own family felt I should get out to California without delay. I was too dazed to protest—and in any case I wasn't sure that I wanted to protest—and I left London a few days after the funeral.

I went into the kitchen to make myself a cup of tea. I found something that looked like a kettle, but nothing that resembled any gas or electric cooker that I was familiar with. The whole place looked like the control room of a power station and I was afraid to turn knobs or press buttons lest I should wake up the whole household. I was even a little nervous of opening the fridge, but I did so without mishap and poured myself a glass of orange juice. I was sitting on a high stool sipping it slowly, when there came a clatter of clogs and Jo appeared in a short nylon dressing-gown over a short nylon nightie, hiding nothing but rather drawing attention to things which, in my household at least, had usually remained hidden. She was not quite as thin as she looked with her clothes on.

'Can't sleep?' she said.

'I've always been an early riser.'

'Nigel isn't. He can sleep all day and sometimes does, but then he sometimes works all night.'

'They film at night?'

'They don't, he works in cabaret.'

'I never knew he was a cabaret artist.'

'He's an everything artist. Coffee?'

She made me a cup and a jug for herself and Nigel and went back to her room. That's what I called a dutiful wife. Dora never brought me tea in bed, not that I would have wanted it. I found it difficult enough to balance a cup of tea standing up, never mind lying back. I drank the coffee, washed, shaved and dressed and took a walk round the neighbourhood, which seemed to consist largely of white concrete villas, ornamented with an occasional iron grill, but which didn't have the solid, sturdy, square, familiar look of English houses. They looked as if they were made out of icing sugar. The lawns were undivided by hedges or fences though bushes and trees here and there provided a bit of privacy. I wanted to buy a paper and though I explored the entire estate—which was extensive—I didn't see a shop of any sort. I felt a little like Alice in Wonderland. 'What is the use of a book without pictures,' and what is the use of a housing estate without shops?

When I got back both Nigel and Jo were up and dressed, or at least Jo was. Nigel was in a flowery blouse and shorts, but I wasn't sure whether they were his pyjamas or some sort of Californian day-wear.

'You don't get sunshine like this in London at this time of the year,' said Nigel.

We didn't. I rather wished we didn't have it here either, for bright sunshine seemed to mock me when I was feeling low, though I wasn't even feeling low; I was feeling dead.

They had a breakfast of fried eggs and pancakes and honeys and syrups and jams, the sight of which nearly turned my stomach. I had coffee and toast and an apple which was about the size of a small melon, but which was almost tasteless.

'That's America all over,' said Nigel, 'appearance and size at the expense of content. You should see the strawberries, big as tomatoes, and beautiful to look at — taste like cotton wool. Americans eat with their eyes.'

After breakfast Jo went off to work in one car and Nigel took me swimming in another. I thought he must have had some distance to go, but it couldn't have been more than five hundred yards.

It seemed wrong to frolic around in a pool in the early hours of a working day of a working month, but there were already twenty or more people in the water.

'Doesn't anybody here work for a living?' I said.

'Sure they do, a darned sight harder than in England — but they don't all work regular hours and they don't all have regular jobs. They're out of work, half of them.' For unemployed they seemed to be living all right.

I floundered around the water half-heartedly and once, when under the water I felt sorely tempted to stay under, only I couldn't do it to Nigel and Jo, or to the children and then it occurred to me with a jolt that I hadn't even made my will. The thought made me come alive, not very much alive, but enough to be getting on with. I had found something to do.

When I got back to the house I got myself a pencil and paper and first tried to work out what I was worth. I had naturally presumed that Dora would survive me and I had taken out a number of insurance policies. Two, which had matured when I was sixty-five, were worth about £20,000 and a third worth about £50,000 would mature when I was seventy. Our house, with furniture and fittings, was worth about £30,000, which was already £100,000 and I had about £200,000 in investments. I hadn't tried to get rich quickly during the boom years on the Stock Exchange, so I didn't grow poor quickly when the boom burst. All my money was in gilt-edged or sound, long-established companies, so I was worth nearly £300,000, perhaps even more. If I dropped now (or did something silly—as I had been tempted to do) most of that would go in death duties. On the other hand if I started distributing it now, I would become dependent on my children, the thought of which was enough to make me drop. My instinct was to divide everything equally among the children, but then their needs weren't equal. Nothing I could leave to Gypsy would add materially to her living standards, though of course it might make her independent and she might think of leaving Nathan and re-marrying. On the other hand had she wanted to leave him she could have done so years ago. She had a profession and could have earned a good salary, and in any case she knew that I would always have helped her if the need arose. I had thought of making special provisions for Nigel, because it didn't occur to me that a comparatively unknown actor could make a living, but with his spacious villa and two cars he seemed to be living better than Arthur and Phyllis who, moreover, had four children.

As I juggled with the figures I felt like a deflated doll in the course of re-inflation and I realised with a slight shock that my depression was due not so much to the death of Dora, as to the fact that I was removed from business. I was rather ashamed of this bit of self-discovery. I liked business and juggling with figures, but it had never occurred to me that I actually lived for business.

I wrote a long letter to my solicitor detailing what I

thought I was worth. I decided that Nigel, as my actual heir, should get a quarter of my estate with a further quarter to be held in reserve in case he should have any children. If not the estate should be divided equally between Nigel and his sisters. It seemed to be the most sensible way of doing things and the most likely way of avoiding recriminations and acrimony and litigation.

Father, though at one time a man of substance, had passed on most of his money during his lifetime, so that there was little left when he died, but his will had been badly drafted and most of what was left went in litigation as sister sued sister and if they hadn't been dramatically brought together by the death of David, one half of the family would not have been on speaking terms with the other.

If it didn't take me long to apportion my estate, I wasn't quite certain when to start apportioning it if only because I didn't know how long I was likely to live. I was not, as Dora frequently reminded me, a big spender—my only indulgence was my fast car (and even that I bought secondhand), but there was no telling how long I would last or how much I would need and, of course, it would depend where I lived.

I asked Nigel how much he spent.

'I don't know. Jo and I earn $60,000—that's about £40,000 and it all goes, but then there's the kids and kids are expensive. A single guy living alone could manage on half that.'

'£20,000 a year?'

'Yes, but that's in California. In England you could get by on £10,000.'

Even £10,000 struck me as a fortune. It would be nice, I thought, if one could deposit a certain sum in the bank and if it expired one expired with it. What began as a pleasant exercise became a troubling one. Supposing I outlived my means and had nothing to leave to my family? Supposing I actually became dependent on them?

Nigel must have noticed I was in something of a state, for he grasped me firmly by an elbow and took me out to lunch. Before leaving he fixed a contraption to the phone.

'An answering machine,' he explained. 'I live and breathe by the phone. I'm waiting for good news and if it doesn't come soon I'll break the fucking thing.'

'What sort of good news?'

'I'll tell you when it comes, if it comes, but Christ, it had better come soon.'

I was unhappy about the slightly desperate tone in his voice.

'You don't seem to be doing too badly now.'

'Bits, bits, bits and pieces, a line here, two lines there, never the part I've been waiting for.'

He sounded a little like a woman on the verge of middle age, desperate to have her first child.

He took me to a Jewish restaurant serving kosher-style food. It was full of tanned, white-haired, leathery men in casual clothes, as if they were all on holiday, which perhaps they were. There wasn't a woman in the place.

The appearance of Nigel caused a stir and whatever his standing in his own eyes he was obviously quite a celebrity in this particular establishment and a waiter appeared at our side with an alacrity I had never known in any Jewish restaurant and it was Mr Newman this and Mr Newman that and Yes, Mr Newman, sir.

'You're more famous than I thought.'

'Sure I am. I told you. You've heard of Peshkin's Pastrami?'

'No.'

'"Pass, pass, pass the Peshkins."' Heard the jingle?'

'No.'

'You ain't heard of Peshkins?'

'No.'

'But you've heard of pastrami?'

'Just about—it's some sort of salt-beef.'

'It's *the* sort of salt-beef, and I'm the pastrami fresser in the Peshkins Pastrami ads, that's why they're all dancing round me. Big deal.'

'I love salt beef.'

'I used to love it, but now that I live on it, I hate the fucking stuff — wouldn't feed it to my dog — throw up every time there's a re-make.'

I wasn't particularly hungry and asked for a smoked-salmon sandwich and got the nearest thing to it which they called beigle and lox. The beigle wasn't like the beigles I had known in London which were small glazed and crisp with a large hole in the middle. These were great puffed-up dimpled rolls, about the size of a small loaf, with caraway seeds on top and what they called smoked salmon — which in London was sliced into thin transparent slivers, was a great, rubbery wedge, like the heel of a man's shoe, only red in colour. I could hardly get my teeth round it, let alone digest it.

'That's America for you,' said Nigel, 'if enough's as good as a feast, too much is better.'

I went to sleep in the afternoon. When I woke I found two small figures contemplating me in the darkened room, one a girl of about ten, the other a boy of about three or four.

'Hullo Zeida,' said the little girl. 'I'm Mo, he's Moishe.'

'What did you call me?' I asked.

'Zeida. It's Ma's idea. She's on to the ethnic kick and she thinks Zeida sounds better than Grandpa.'

# 3

Zeida! That was something we had called grandfather, but he had looked a Zeida, an ancient, stooping figure, half-blind, wholly deaf and with a white beard. And here the same appellation was being applied to me, but it was not merely the idea of being thought of as an ancient which startled me, but the sound of Yiddish in a Californian accent. What would mother have made of it?

Jo later explained that she was taking Yiddish lessons.

'Yiddish lessons!' I said, 'We were discouraged from staying with our grandparents in case we should bring Yiddish back with us. I was half brought up to think that it was some kind of plague.'

'What a pity, you could have taught it to me. Yiddish is beautiful, it has resonance, flavour, colour. It's ethnic.'

'It's crap,' said Nigel.

'You see what I mean? Always negative. No pride in his heritage.'

'I'm afraid it's my fault,' I said, 'I didn't give him much of a pride in his heritage.'

'Neither did my parents, I hardly knew I was Jewish, but about the time I was expecting Moishe I began to think—'

'That's why he's called Moishe,' put in Mo. 'My name's Maureen.'

'Pregnancies do make you contemplative,' said Jo. 'You've got this whole world building up inside you and you begin to think what am I going to do with it? What am I letting it in for? You feel safer with an attachment to the past. We have so many things to be proud of and they go so far back. There are people in America who take great pride in tracing their families back to the Mayflower, who were never within a hundred years of the Mayflower. Well, my family goes back to the Ark.'

'So does everybody's family,' said Nigel. 'Now let's have something to eat.'

'See what I mean?' said Jo in my ear. 'Negative.'

'If you want to rediscover your heritage,' I said, 'why don't you learn Hebrew?'

'Hebrew? Hebrew's a bit political, isn't it? I like the sound of Yiddish, it's more ethnic.'

'Do you know what she's talking about?' asked Mo, 'because I don't.' She was a thin, unsmiling little girl with pigtails and wire-rimmed glasses. Moishe, a squat little figure with a large head as round as a cannonball was still trying to work out my place in his firmament and by the look of him I was not welcome.

I helped to put him to bed. He had a room of his own which was crammed with toys like a toy shop, great fluffy bears bigger than he was, giraffes, rabbits, wooden toys, hydraulic engines, plastic toys, cars, buses, tanks, aeroplanes, rockets, revolvers, rifles, machine-guns, rocket-launchers, space capsules, a hobby horse, inflatable monsters, a battery-operated Donald Duck, remote-controlled railway engines. I spent half an hour playing with them myself, until Moishe objected.

'They're not yours,' he said, 'they're mine.'

'I'm just trying them out to see how they work.'

'They're not yours.'

'I'm not saying they are.'

'They're mine.'

'All right, they're yours.'

'Put them down.'

I put them down.

'You mustn't touch them.'

Jo smiled apologetically. 'Not having a father is a dreadful trauma for a small child and it's made him sort of like he is.'

'But he's got two fathers.'

'Yes, but neither father is completely his and two half-fathers don't really add up to a whole one.'

'He touched my Donald.'

'I know he has darling, but he's put him down.'

'He shouldn't have touched him.'

'He won't do it again, sugar.'

'I was only seeing how it worked.'

'They don't have these things in England, sugar, they're deprived.'

'I don't want him to touch Donald.'
'I won't.'
'You see, Zeida promised he won't do it again.'
'He shouldn't have touched him.'
'I'll tell you what, I'll buy you a new one.'
'There, Zeida will buy you a new one—would you like that?'
'I want a new Donald *and* a new Goofy.'
'A new what?'
'Goofy. Don't you go to the movies?'
'Goofy? Yes, Micky Mouse. The children loved him.'
'Moishe loves him too, but I don't believe in giving kids everything they want, they should sort of feel they've earned it by some sort of sacrifice, don't you?'
'Yes, but if he's upset—'
'Yes, he is, poor darling. I suppose that is a sacrifice. Did you hear sugar? Zeida's going to buy you a Goofy.'
'And a Donald.'
'And a Donald.'
'And Pluto.'
'No, no Pluto.'
'Yes, Pluto.'
'Moishe, you don't want Mummy to be upset.'
'I want Pluto.'
'Mummy's going to be upset, sugar.'
I began to say something, but she cut me short.
'No Zeida, I don't want you to indulge him. Enough's enough. You touched his Donald so you are compensating him with Goofy. There is no call for Pluto as well. I don't even know if they have an electronic Pluto.'
'I was going to suggest that he may be tired.'
'No, it's your intrusion, Zeida. He thinks you want to take his place in my affection and wants compensation, but I don't believe in over-compensating.'
'Why don't you kick him?' said Mo.
Jo gave me a troubled glance, but said nothing.
'I think Mo is an incipient lesbian,' she told me later. 'If

Moishe wakes in the night I take him into my bed—he has a
healthy Oedipal instinct—but Mo would obviously like to
take his place. It's the absence of a father, you see. If she
had a father she would, of course, want to sleep with him,
which is perfectly natural, but in the absence of a father she
sublimates her instincts in me.'

One evening when Moishe was undressing I noticed that
he had an odd little garment under his shirt, made of cotton
or nylon, with long woollen fringes in each corner and I was
moved by curiosity to ask what it was.

'You mean you've never seen one before?' said Jo.

'No.'

And she went to her room and brought back a large,
black Bible and began to read:

And the Lord spake unto Moses saying. Speak unto the
children of Israel and bid them that they make them
fringes in the borders of their garments throughout their
generations and that they put upon the fringe of the
borders a riband of blue. And it shall be unto you for a
fringe, that you may look upon it and remember all the
commandments of the Lord and do them; and that ye
seek not after your own heart and your own eyes, after
which ye used to go a-whoring.

'It's all there. Never heard it before?'

'Yes, but I thought it only referred to prayer shawls—'

'Well, the prayer shawl is only a larger version of this and
you know it has a prophylactic factor—'

'A what?'

'It's protective. Moishe used to get all sorts of illnesses.
There was hardly a month in which he wasn't down with
something, but he's been wearing these and he's been fine.'

'Does Mo wear one too?'

'No, these commandments only apply to boys. Judaism,
like all the ancient religions, is male-dominated; but I think
domination is a good thing as long as it's by mutual consent,

don't you? People like to be dominated. Mo used to wear a little "mezuzah" round her neck.'

'A "mezuzah"? I thought that was something you had on door posts.'

'They're mandatory on door posts, but you can wear them round your neck too. Unfortunately she developed a skin allergy against metal and had to stop it.'

'Do you keep all the commandments?'

'I try to. I never take the Lord's name in vain. I honour my mother—if you knew my mother, you'd see that was no easy thing, for she's nutty as a fruit cake. It would have been easier to honour my father, but he's dead. I remember the Sabbath day and keep it holy—after a fashion. I don't work on the Sabbath, but I have to travel because everything's miles from anywhere and you'd be a prisoner in your own home if you didn't. I don't kill, I don't steal, oh and I have no other Gods before me, and I don't bear false witness, I do gossip, but that isn't the same thing is it? That's seven out of ten, isn't it, which isn't bad for someone who, until C. B. de Mille, wasn't sure what the Ten Commandments were.'

'Do you covet your neighbour's ass?'

'Not even his Cadillac, but I do covet his menservants and his maidservants. They're so difficult to get and so expensive to keep.'

'Do you keep kosher?'

'We don't eat pork or shell fish, if that's what you mean.'

'That I don't eat myself, but do you get your meat from a kosher butcher?'

'I did once, but it's so tasteless. They drain the meat and salt it and water it, till it's washed out—it's got no flavour. Nigel said it's not fit for a dog. I believe in ethnicity, but if you study the history of Jewish food you will see it's not really Jewish. It's Russian or Polish, or Hungarian, or German or Spanish—depending on where they happened to be and it's so rich in calories and cholesterol.'

'Rich in what?'

'Cholesterol, poison. Jewish food's full of it. Somebody's

worked it out that if it wasn't for the typical Jewish food
eaten by the typical Jew there would be over two hundred
million Jews in the world today. It's a form of birth control
really, Jewish food, only post-natal. I have to watch Nigel
like a hawk, for he loves poison, butter, whipped cream,
chopped liver.'

'Chopped liver and whipped cream?'

'Not at the same time, but whenever my back's turned
he'll have his eggs fried in butter, his fish cooked in butter—
it's a suppressed death wish. I don't allow butter in the
house, but he smuggles it in and hides it in odd corners
everywhere—it's like having a secret alcoholic in the house,
except that butter turns rancid, so he's always found out.
I'm always surprised that the Torah, which is so right about
so many things, hasn't banned butter. Do you know your son
well?'

'About as well as any father knows his child.'

She lowered her voice and looked around her.

'Nigel has a butter fixation.'

'A what?'

'A butter fixation. Did he have a difficult delivery?'

'You mean when he was born?'

'Yes, did he have a smooth passage?'

'He had a big head which caused no end of trouble.'

'That's it. That explains it. I thought it may have had
something to do with his first wife, she had a dry vagina, you
know.'

'I didn't.'

'Bone dry, but his difficult birth is more likely. He
obviously has some pathological fear of obstructions and
butter, of course, symbolises a smooth passage.'

What was developing into an embarrassing conversation
was cut short by the phone. Jo dived on it.

'Yes, yes, hullo. Yes. It is. Yes. No. Yes. I see. What? Yes.'
Her voice and face fell. Whatever she was waiting for hadn't
materialised. The whole household was neurotic about the
phone. It reminded me of the time when David was ill in

hospital and every time the phone rang we turned to stone, but then we were standing by for the worst and what is bad about the worst is that it has a habit of materialising. Here they were standing by for good news and the bad thing about good news is that it often doesn't come.

'Things just don't seem to be coming right,' she said tearfully. 'He's very gifted, you know—Nigel—very. A genius. He's a marvellous character actor. He sometimes does and says terrible things, but you have to forgive him, for he gets so deep into the part he forgets himself—that's why I'd never let him play Dracula. It nearly came to it once and I told him I'm going back to mother with the children until the shooting's over. Being with mother is no joy, but it's better than being with Dracula. Thank God it fell through. I was praying it would. I keep asking his agent why can't they ever cast him as hero, I don't mean in the Gary Cooper sort of role, he hasn't got the height, but say, for example, St Francis—'

'He hasn't got the face.'

'It doesn't have to be a saint, it could be a Rabbi, but it's almost always a bad man, and a low sort of bad man at that and when he gets into the part he doesn't wash, he doesn't shave, he doesn't change his underwear, he's impossible to live with. You don't know what I went through when he played a rapist, but you make allowances for genius and he is a genius—the greatest character actor since Wallace Beery, only more versatile. He can sing, dance—'

'Dance?' I said incredulously.

'I don't mean ballet dancing, but he's like a feather on his feet and he's a great comedian. You know I think they're anti-Semites.'

'Who?'

'The movie and television chiefs.'

'But they're all Jews, aren't they?'

'So they're Jewish anti-Semites. They've no feel for ethnicity and they don't know talent when they see it. When he was in London he met this producer and by chance he thought he had the very part for him and he said he'd confirm it in a day or two. Well, it's almost a week or two and he hasn't phoned yet and when you get—'

She was interrupted by Moishe who came between us demanding:

'Don't talk to him. Talk to me.'

'I was only explaining something, sugar.'

'I don't want you to explain something to him, explain something to me.'

'A minute, sugar.'

'No, not a minute, now.'

'Now Moishe, honey, you don't want your mamma to be upset with you.'

'Don't talk to him, talk to *me*.'

'See how sensitive he is? He feels my upset, so he's upset— he's like that all the time, he connects to my worries. I know I'm an ingrate, but I sometimes wish I had less sensitive children.'

I was to share her wishes. She had a Yiddish class that evening and she rushed out asking if I could put the children to bed.

'Moishe has his lights out at eight and Mo at nine,' she cried over her shoulder.

Mo was sitting cross-legged on her bed drinking a Coke, picking her nose and watching television as I came into her room.

'What are you watching?' I asked.

'Crap.'

'Then why are you watching it?'

'Because I like crap.'

'Well, it's well after nine dear, so I had better switch off.' She raised no objections, but as soon as I was out of the room she switched on again.

'Your mother said—' I began.

'I know what she said. Well, you're doing what you were told to do and I'm doing what I want to do. Good night.'

'Do you think that's sensible?'

'It makes sense to me.'

'You've got school tomorrow. You'll hardly be able to get up early if you're in bed late, or to concentrate on your work. Your mother does know what's best for you.'

'She doesn't even know what's best for herself,' she said, without diverting her gaze from the screen. 'If you're passing this way again, can you get me another Coke?'

I left it at that, though I didn't get her another Coke, which would have meant total surrender and in any case I soon had Moishe on my hands. I had switched off the lights in his room, with slight trepidation at the thought of the tantrums which might ensue, but a little to my surprise there were none. About an hour or two later, however, I was in my own room trying to see what there was on television, when there came a thud of footsteps in the corridor (whoever spoke of 'the patter' of tiny feet could never have had children) and he was in the doorway.

'What are you watching?'

'What are you doing out of bed, young man?'

'What are you watching?'

'Television.'

'I know you're watching television, dummy, but what programme?'

'I think you had better go straight to bed.'

'I want to watch.'

'You can't.'

'Then why are you watching?'

'Moishe, honey you don't want your Zeida to be upset with you, do you?'

'I wanna watch.'

I switched off the set. 'There, I'm not watching either. Now will you go to bed?'

'I wanna drink.'

I took him to the bathroom and poured him a glass of water.

'No, not water.'

'In which case you can't be very thirsty.'

'I am very thirsty.'

'Then you'll have water.'

'I DON'T WANT WATER!' he said in a scream out of all proportion to his size.

'In which case you're not having anything.'

'Yes I am.'

'No, you're not.'

'Yes I am.'

'No, you're not.'

'YES I AM.'

'You'd better go to bed young man, before I give you a spanking.'

'What's a spanking?'

'I'll take off your pyjamas and hit you very hard across your bottom.'

'You mean like Mummy does to Daddy?'

'I—straight to bed now, and no nonsense.'

'No.'

'Do you want a hard smack across your bottom?'

He retreated at that, but still insisted on a drink.

'You're not getting a drink.'

'I am.'

'You're not.'

'I AM.'

'He gets a malted milk, Zeida!' shouted Mo from her room.

'He had a malted milk before he went to bed!' I shouted back.

'He has another.'

'I have another,' he repeated, with a glint of triumph in his eyes.

'Over my dead body,' I said and for the first time appreciated why infanticide was so commonplace.

'I wanna malted milk.'

'You're not getting a malted milk.'

'I am.'

'You're not.'

'I AM.'

'You raise your voice once more young man and I'll give you such a smack you won't know what hit you.' He raised his voice again and I gave him a whack across his bottom which half dislocated my wrist and which left him standing there paralysed for a moment, his mouth open, his eyes grown large, trying to work out if what he thought had happened really had happened. When it became clear that it had, he let out a yowl like a cat being skinned alive. It went through my head like a spike and Mo came sauntering into the room to see what was wrong.

'Have you killed him?' she asked.

'No.'

'Pity,' she said and left.

But the yowling continued and I could do nothing to staunch the noise or the tears and he only quietened down after he had shouted himself hoarse, by which time I had made him a large mug of malted milk, but he was too tired to touch it and dropped off to sleep.

Jo returned a minute later.

'All quiet?' she asked sweetly.

'All quiet.'

'I don't know how you do it, Zeida, it takes me hours to get them to sleep. I think I'll have you here as a permanent nanny. No phone calls?'

'None.'

Her face fell again. 'Poor Nigel. I sometimes wish he wasn't a genius and had a nine to five job like the rest of us. I don't like him being away at this hour of the night. Terrible things happen in California—they happen everywhere, but they happen more often in California and a woman needs a man under her roof for more reasons than one. I never really get to sleep till he's back. A woman needs someone to rub against—it sort of makes her feel secure.'

'Well,' I said quickly, 'it's long past my bed time.'

'Zeida?'

'Yes.'

'Kiss me good night.'

I kissed her on the forehead. She had a lovely smooth, warm, taut skin.

'Only there?'

And I kissed her on the cheek.

'You're not giving me a medal, Zeida, I want a proper kiss.' And she put her arms round me and kissed me on the lips.

Mo, who unseen to us, had come into the kitchen, later explained:

'She never had a father, you know; she's got a delayed Oedipus complex.'

# 4

A few days later I was wakened in the early hours of the morning by the sound of the phone. I sat bolt upright and groped for a switch. It was ten to five. In my experience a call at that hour of the morning could only be bad news. I had an unhappy feeling that it was for me and in the course of a few seconds every calamity which could possibly befall a man with children and grandchildren rushed through my mind. I could hear Nigel's loud excited voice (it reminded me so much of Dora) and then, what seemed like the sound of jubilation.

I put on my dressing-gown and slippers and found Nigel and Jo embracing each other ecstatically in the kitchen.

The goods news I thought had obviously come. It wasn't the good news they'd been waiting for, but it was good enough. One of the leading players in a film being shot in

Spain had fractured a leg and Nigel was asked to take his place.

'Ah,' said Nigel, 'my big break.'

We breakfasted on champagne which, though not quite my cup of tea, was preferable to the pancakes and syrup they usually had and an hour later he was off.

'Things are beginning to go our way,' said Jo. 'Waiting for London's been getting him down. It's been getting me down. But you know, I hate to see him go. L.A. is no place for a young woman to be left on her own—not with two small kids. Thank God you're here.'

A few days later schools and kindergartens broke up for the holidays. Jo still had her own work to go to and I was left in charge of the children.

The first morning passed without mishap, but I had some slight difficulty over lunch. Jo had left out a large tray covered with silver foil which she had told me to bung in the oven an hour before lunch, which I did and when I took it out and peeled off the foil, it turned out to be an exotic-looking pizza. I quite liked it, but Mo said it was crap (which was what she said about everything), but she was no bother because she prepared something else for herself. Moishe was rather more of a problem.

'I want meat balls,' he demanded.

'Your mummy said you should have pizza and this pizza looks delicious and I am going to have some right now.' He watched me eat a slice impassively.

'I want meat balls and a coke,' he said.

'You're going to have pizza or nothing.'

'I want meat balls and a Coke and a banana split.'

'All right then, no lunch for you, I'll have this pizza all to myself.'

'I wouldn't,' said Mo, 'it'll louse up your guts.'

'Mo's having a Coke.'

'But she's not having meat balls.'

'She's not having pizza either.'

He was too clever by half and I felt like dumping the pizza

on his big round head. Instead I turned helplessly to Mo.

'What does your mother do in such a situation?'

'She gives in.'

I wasn't going to start cooking him meat balls (even if I knew how) and his lunch finally consisted of Coca Cola, potato crisps and ice cream, not a particularly nourishing diet, but he seemed sufficiently nourished as it was. I finished off most of the pizza and, as Mo warned, it loused up my guts, but not permanently.

After lunch I suggested an airing and we hadn't gone five yards when Moishe stopped.

'Where are we going?'

'For a walk.'

'Then why aren't you taking the car?'

'How can you walk if you take the car, stupid?' said Mo.

'I don't wanna walk.'

'I haven't got a car,' I said.

'Use Daddy's car.'

'Your Daddy didn't say I could use it.'

'I say you can use it.'

'I don't want to use it. I want to walk.'

'I don't wanna walk.'

'I do.'

'I don't.'

'All right then, you can stay at home and Mo and I will go by ourselves.'

'I wanna go in the car.'

'You're not going in the car.'

'I am.'

'You're not.'

'I AM,' and he stamped his foot, with little effect, however, for we were on the lawn.

'All right then, bye-bye.'

And Mo and I walked on a little, leaving him behind.

'It's no good,' said Mo, 'he knows you're fooling.'

'But I'm not giving in to him.'

'You will, everybody does.'

'Let's walk on another bit.' And we walked on about another fifty yards and hid behind a bush so we could be out of sight.

'You'll see, he'll soon come and look for us.'

'He won't.'

He didn't and instead, after waiting fruitlessly for some minutes, we went to look for him, by which time he had vanished.

'He's been kidnapped,' said Mo hopefully.

I raced round the garden like a headless hen, calling for him at the top of my voice. We then tried the house, room by room, even the cupboards, still shouting his name. He was nowhere. We tried the garden again, the garage, the shrubberies, but he was nowhere.

'Moishe! Moishe! Moishe!' Our voices fell flat in the hot air. There wasn't even an answering echo. I was sweating and my shirt stuck to my back like an outer skin. I sat down to wipe my brow and take stock.

We hadn't left him out of sight for more than five minutes, so he couldn't have got far and as Mo added reassuringly, he had been brought up in the belief that legs were for indoor use only and never walked more than ten yards at a time if he could help it. Yet we had searched the entire radius he could have covered and had found no sign of him. It was as if the earth had opened and swallowed him up. Could he have been picked up? A car had passed nearby. The more I thought the more jittery I became. I ran to Nigel's car — with no clear certainty of what I would do next and my hand was so shaky it took me a minute or two to get the key into the ignition and I was just backing out of the garage when a car pulled up. It was Jo.

'Where are you going?'

'Moishe's missing,' said Mo laconically.

'Moishe,' screamed Jo. Before she could recover her voice a young woman appeared from next door, leading Moishe by the hand.

'I found him on his own and I got nervous,' she explained.

Jo was still shaking several hours and I don't know how many tranquillisers later.

'Anything could have happened to him. He's only four. He could have been strangled, kidnapped, raped. Nobody leaves a child of any age unattended in L.A. There are psychopaths everywhere. And it's full of swimming pools, he could have wandered in and got drowned. I know he's not your own grandchild, but would you have left your own four-year-old grandchild unattended like that?'

'We left him for a minute, we were only playing.'

'Well I'm sorry if you play that sort of game in England, we don't in America. You know what this means don't you? I can't leave you in charge of the children any more.'

I felt like pointing out that I hadn't actually asked to be left in charge, but she continued:

'Laureen nearly fainted when she saw him standing there, nobody in the house, nobody in sight, all on his own, poor little mouse.' And she turned in a fury on Mo. 'How could you let him do it?'

'Let who do what?'

'How could you let him leave poor little Moishe out on his own? You know the sort of things that go on here. Did you want your baby brother to be strangled?'

She was non-committal.

'Couldn't you have warned Zeida?'

'Nothing happened to him.'

'Nothing happened to him because I've got trustworthy neighbours. Supposing Laureen hadn't looked out and found him?'

'Then we wouldn't have lost him.'

'Thank God for Laureen. I don't know what I'd have done without her. A child of his age was strangled in the San Fernando Valley only last month. He was left unattended for a minute. This is L.A., everything's on wheels, things happen quickly. Five minutes. Whole families have been slaughtered in five minutes.'

'Look, perhaps I'm too old to cope with children their age.'

'You obviously are, but I don't know what I'll do. I can't leave my work and Nigel's away for another month.'

'Can't one get child-minders or something?'

'They're unobtainable, unrealiable and too expensive. I had one last year, Mexican and she actually hit Moishe. Can you imagine it, hitting a poor child of three? A sadist. I was in two minds whether to call the police.'

'Well as a matter of fact I hit Moishe.'

She looked at me with disbelief.

'You?'

'Yes.'

'Hit?'

'Yes.'

'Moishe?'

'Yes, hard, across his backside.'

'When?'

'Last week.'

She looked at Mo for confirmation.

'Did he?'

'He didn't spill no blood.'

'Did he hit Moishe?'

'If he says he did, I guess he did.'

She strode out of the room without another word and I went quietly to mine and began to pack, but then it occurred to me that she was probably on the phone to Nigel at that very minute telling him there was a crisis at home and asking him to come back. She was a stupid and neurotic woman and beside herself and I didn't want her to jeopardise Nigel's career (what there was of it). I hoped that he had the strength of character not to let her and that he could stand up to her better than I stood up to Dora, but I wasn't sure. He was, after all, my son even if he had the shape and sound of his mother. There was only one thing to be done. I had to go back to Jo, apologise and assure her I wouldn't do it again. I would choke the child with meat balls and banana-splits and everything would be all right.

But then I asked myself what would have happened if I

hadn't come out in the first place. Nigel wouldn't have said no to the opportunity and she would either have had to stay home or hire someone to look after the children. I resumed my packing. I was an independent individual, with a life of my own. My children were old enough to work out their own problems and I wasn't too old to work out mind. I would fly back tomorrow.

There was a hesitant knock at the door. I ignored it and it came louder.

'Who is it?'

'It's me,' said Jo, sounding very contrite. I opened.

'I'm sorry. The kids are everything to me and I always go like that when I think of what could have happened — you've no idea of the things that actually do happen. I'm sorry, I should have remembered your age.'

'Forgive me, but what has my age to do with it?'

'You've got to be young to handle young children. My mother wasn't any better. I could never leave the children with her. Mo yes, Moishe never.'

'Has it ever occurred to you that Moishe is perhaps a little er — ' I searched for a euphemism.

'Sensitive?'

'No, that isn't the word.'

'Difficult?'

'Well, yes.'

'But remember his age and his circumstances. He's no angel, I realise that, but all he needs is a little patience and understanding and, of course, acceptance. He is a very sensitive child, *very* sensitive and if he senses anything negative in your attitude, then it's all over, you can't do anything with him. But if you show patience, understanding, love you'll never find an easier child — happy, playful, co-operative, affectionate, a joy. But of course, people don't always have patience when they get to a certain age. My mother wouldn't have Moishe in the house and she's not even seventy.'

The way she said *not even seventy*, made me suspect that she thought I was in my eighties.

'Anyway, whatever happened, I should never have lost my temper with you even if I was in the right. If we can't respect our elders, what is there left of our Jewishness? I am sorry. I'll have somebody in to look after them.'

'That won't be necessary.'

'Of course it will. It was thoughtless of me to leave a man of your age all day in the house with two small children.'

'Will you not go on about my age, I'm not senile.'

' I am not suggesting you are. In fact you're an attractive, well-preserved man, but patience is the first faculty to go.'

'Yes, but I was thrown in at the deep end, without warning. Now I know what the situation is I should be able to handle it.'

'You say that now, but what'll happen if you lose your temper?'

'I didn't lose my temper—'

'You mean you hit him in cold blood?'

'I—look, I hit Nigel in cold blood, not often enough or hard enough, perhaps, but I did hit him.'

'That explains a lot.'

'Do you never hit your children?'

'*Hit* a child? Of *that* age? It's all right, I'll have somebody in to look after them.'

'I shan't raise a finger to them—Scout's honour.'

'You don't take me seriously. Nigel's the same. I don't know if he takes himself seriously, but he doesn't take me seriously at all.'

'I give you my word of honour I shan't raise a finger to them.'

'I'll tell you what, I'll leave you my number and if there are any difficulties, phone me, but please, please don't hit them. It's not that you may fracture something, that can always be repaired. It's what you may do to their sub-conscious.'

'I shan't come within a mile of their subconscious.'

To cut a long story short, she left me to look after them and things went without a hitch. I found that as long as I had Moishe in a moving vehicle and as long as he had something in his hand to suck or to chew or to crunch or slurp, he was no trouble at all, although he turned green from time to time and every now and again vomited on the car floor. I don't know what it all did to his teeth or his cholesterol intake. It certainly didn't do much good to the car, but the time went quickly and I was able to see quite a bit of California and Arizona. I found it quite interesting, for I didn't mind torrents of traffic as long as they moved and they did move, while the landscape was varied and exciting; but poor Mo was bored. She had been everywhere and seen everything.

'Dad gypped on Ma so he's trying to make up to us and every Sunday it's some place new.'

I never, in fact, saw their mysterious dad, for a large car arrived on Sunday morning to collect the children and returned in the evening to bring them back. Apparently that was something worked out between the lawyers. Jo didn't want to set eyes on him. Sunday, therefore, was my day off and it was on one such Sunday that I received a phone call from New York.

At first I couldn't make out the voice or the name, possibly because I didn't associate either with New York. It was Iris.

'Iris! Good God, what are you doing here?'

'Business. Would you like to see me?'

'That's a silly question.'

'You mean you wouldn't.'

'Of course I would—any chance of you coming out here?'

'I could for a day or so.'

She arrived two days later and Mo, Moishe and I drove out to the airport to meet her. I wasn't quite sure how to greet her, whether to throw my arms round her, or what? I'm not a natural arms-thrower as it is and the presence of Mo and Moishe settled that. Iris herself seemed a little distant and gave me a sisterly kiss.

'Who is that?' Moishe demanded.

'That's Auntie Iris, I told you all about her before.'

'Is she Dad's sister?'

'No.'

'Is she Mummy's sister?'

'No.'

'Then how is she an auntie?'

'She's Zeida's date, stupid,' said Mo in a whisper.

'I don't like her, I want her to go away.'

That continued for much of the day and it was not till the evening, when I was driving Iris to her hotel, that I had a chance to speak with her.

'I suppose you're wondering why I came out here?'

'I'd have been upset if you hadn't, once you were in America.'

'Didn't they teach you geography at school? It takes as long to get from New York to California as from London to New York.'

'I know, but once you're on the move, you move that bit further. In any case, Scandawools must be doing very well if they can send you to New York. I never travelled further than Finland. I never even dreamed of establishing an American connection.'

'We are doing very well, which is another reason why it wasn't all that easy for me to come here, but I managed to snatch a day off.'

When we got to her hotel, she went upstairs to wash and change while I waited in the cocktail bar. This was my second or third experience of American cocktail bars and I didn't care for them. They always seem to be in almost complete darkness, as if people were afraid to be seen there and they seemed to be designed for furtive assignations rather than for something as convivial as a drink and when Iris came towards me it took me time to make out who she was.

I spent a long time asking her questions about Scanda-wools and its personnel and she was always laconic in her replies, as if not anxious to continue the topic, or rather because she was impatient to get on to a more pressing issue.

I had more than a vague idea what the issue would be, which was perhaps why I kept pressing her about Scandawools, and she finally cut me short and pulled a letter from her handbag.

'I think you should see this.'

I couldn't read it in the almost complete darkness.

'Shall we go up to my room? You'll be safe, it's en suite.'

It was, in fact, a bedroom, bathroom and a lounge. I had never in my life stayed in such luxury. I opened the letter. It was from Dora:

Dear Iris,

Letters isn't my strong point because if I have anything to say I say it and I don't think I've written more than five or six letters in my life, but I don't know if I'll ever have the chance to see you and in any case what I have to say should be put on paper, so I'm writing this and leaving it with my solicitor who will send it to you after my death, which may be next week, or next month, but which can't be long.

I haven't many precious possessions. I've got a few bits of jewels and things which I'm leaving to my children and grandchildren, but I think I also owe something to you and I should like to leave you my husband, Sidney Newman. I spoke to him about it a few weeks ago and he laughed and said I'd outlive you all. He was wrong, of course, and you'll see how wrong he is when you get this letter. He's had to put up with a lot from his mother for the first thirty or so years of his life and then from me from the next thirty-five. He's still got a good ten or fifteen years of life left in him and I would like him to enjoy it in good company. I may be a dying woman, but I'm not a senile one and I wouldn't have written this if I hadn't known that you were fond of him and he of you and if I hadn't thought you could be very happy together.

Yours,<br>Dora.

'It's her tidiness,' I explained. 'She liked to leave everything in its place and neatly tied up and didn't like the idea of leaving me at a loose end.'

'You don't look as if you're at a loose end. I saw you with your daughter-in-law earlier in the evening and you seem to have worked out a very cosy relationship.'

'She's a sweet child and very hospitable.'

'I'm sure she is, but did you notice the looks she kept shooting in my direction? Not hostile, but enquiring, trying to work out our relationship.'

'I told her you were my secretary.'

'I know, but ex-secretaries don't travel three thousand miles to see their ex-boss, though I might as well tell you why I did come out — not to claim the pound of flesh bequeathed by your wife, so you can set your mind at rest there — but I have an obsession about your family and perhaps you in particular — which has stopped me from forming any lasting relationship. It began, of course, with David. He was taller than you and better-looking, which, I think, gave him more self-assurance, though he had less to be self-assured about, because you had the better head and firmer personality, but you are alike in many ways, in gestures, in temperament, in manner of speaking and I suppose when he died I transferred my affections to you and through you to your whole family. I was aware of that but I was hoping that the shock of Dora's death, but more than her death, the attempt to freeze me out, might cauterise my feelings.'

'Have they?'

'I wish I could be sure.'

'Do you want to marry me?'

'Are you proposing, or are you asking out of simple curiosity? You probably don't know yourself. Supposing I said "yes"?'

'I'd marry you.'

'There's Dora asserting her wishes even beyond the grave. You're a good man, Sidney, a kosher St Francis. You'd do anything out of a sense of duty, even marry a shiksa. You

don't really want to marry me. I'm no longer even sure that
David wanted to marry me, but he felt he owed it to me and
you feel you owe it to your wife. I wish I hadn't shown you
her letter. I wish I hadn't come. I wish I was as sensible in
life as I am in business.' She seemed near to tears.

I put a hand on her knees.

'No Sidney, that won't help, you'd better go.'

'Haven't you often said that Dora had more insight than
the two of us? She may be right.'

'I like your "may be", so you suggest we should marry in
case perhaps she was. There's passion for you, there's
enthusiasm.'

'I don't know what you expect me to say.'

'I don't expect you to say anything. I just want you to go.'

'I—'

'I said go.'

'I don't like seeing you upset.'

'Fuck off.'

5

I perhaps had more reason than anyone to greet the return
of Nigel with relief.

I had been in California for nearly three months and I
had had enough. I liked the place itself and had become
almost inured to the kids, but I had had enough. I had
nothing to do with myself and the best place to do it was
England where, at least, I had worked out some sort of
routine like calling on the doctor or gossiping with

Michaelson. I could even take up Telfer's invitation to visit the British Legion.

Jo had prepared a festive banquet to greet her returning hero, and we all went to collect him at the airport, but as soon as we caught sight of him we knew that his trip had been less than a triumph.

'This is gonna be a hell of a day,' whispered Mo.

Jo greeted him with a hug and a kiss and he almost pushed her aside, and dived into the car.

'How was it honey?' said Jo with an effort at cheerfulness.

'Don't ask,' said Mo out of the side of her mouth.

'These eternal blue skies can get on anybody's nerves,' I said.

Nigel sulked in the corner all the way home. It was like going to a funeral with the corpse sitting upright in one's midst.

A day or two passed before it became clear what had happened.

He had indeed been asked to stand in for the main player (a man for whose talents he had the utmost contempt), but the director was not too happy about his ability to fill his place and the part was so written down as to be almost written out.

'It'll teach me self-respect,' said Nigel. 'I shan't stand in again, not even for Elizabeth Taylor.' I was proud of his resilience.

One evening we were all together in the lounge watching a film about some Mexican war in which Jo said Nigel had a major part. We all sat there expectantly with cans of Coca-Cola in our hands, but the moment he appeared on screen he jumped to his feet and put a boot through the tube. There was a flash, a loud bang, glass flew in all directions and the children screamed, while he rushed out of the house with Jo calling after him at the top of her voice.

I got the children to bed and they went silently and without protest. I suspected they were used to such scenes. I then cleared up the debris in the lounge and went into the

kitchen to make a cup of tea. A few minutes later Jo
returned leading the whimpering Nigel by the hand.

Jo was up early the next morning after what looked like a
sleepless night and I said to her:

'You know this can't go on. One day he'll kill himself.'

'Do you think he hasn't tried?' At which I lost my temper.

'But what the hell for? So that he could go on being the
famous pastrami fresser?'

'He's never had the break he deserves.'

'Has it ever occurred to you that he never will and that
most people never do.'

'Sure it's occurred to me and to him, that's why he's like
that. Haven't you noticed, he doesn't even jump on the
phone any more. He's beaten.'

Nigel must have been under sedation for he slept most of
the day, but in the evening when the children were in bed
and Jo was out, we were able to have the sort of father-to-son
conversation we hadn't had in years. He sounded very contrite, less American and more English (perhaps it is difficult
to sound contrite in an American accent).

'Jo tells me you've given up waiting for that call from
London.'

'I've more or less given everything up, or rather, it's given
me up.'

'As a matter of interest, why don't you phone London?'

'Have you never heard of the show-biz catch-phrase "Don't
call us, we'll call you"? It's more than a catch-phrase, it's the
fundamental law of show-biz life. Once you've got to make
the calls, it's over. Though, of course, it is over, I realise that.'

'So what next?'

'I'm nearly forty. I'm moving into the coronary age. A
timely heart attack could solve everything. I'm well insured.'

'Has it occurred to you that you may have taken —'

'The wrong road? If I have it's too late to turn back.'

'But not too late to turn to something new. I was only
about your age when I began in business after the war.'

'You didn't have my track record of failure.'

'I didn't have a track record. Before the war I helped out in father's place doing odd jobs, but he more or less sold out to get my sisters married. I started from scratch.'

'And you're suggesting I do the same, that I start in business at my age?'

'I keep telling you, I was nearly your age.'

'I've got no capital.'

'I have.'

'You don't know the sort of money you need to start up here—'

'You don't know the sort of money I've got.'

'Fifty thousand—a hundred?'

'About half a million dollars.'

'Half—from that tuppenny-halfpenny—'

'You keep calling it that. I was supporting fifty families and if you had gone into the company—but let's not go into that. I should like to start again, but I need a partner.'

'I couldn't go back—'

'I don't mean in London. When I sold out I undertook not to go into the same line of business in competition with Scandawools, but that was of course in Britain. There's nothing to stop me from starting afresh in America, except age, of course. Sixty-seven isn't thirty-seven, but if I had you as a partner—'

'It would be your experience, your contacts, your money, what would I add?'

'Youth, energy, drive.'

'Stop it, Dad, I've got none of these things. I'm beat.'

'At the moment, but you'll recover and the new life'll speed your recovery. We couldn't fail.'

'Couldn't we? Failure becomes a habit. Why don't you bring Iris over?'

'Everyone keeps throwing Iris at me. She's not an indentured slave. She's got a life of her own, with a job of her own and is doing very well thank you.'

'Advertise for a partner. You'd do well, but not with me weighing you down.'

'You're a good actor, you'd make a great salesman. Salesmen have to be actors.'

'And actors have to be salesmen, which is why I've never made it. No, Dad, I wish you luck, but you're better off without me.'

'Then forget it. I can't start on my own and I'm too old to start with people I don't know. And in any case, what makes you think you're a failure? You're a public figure. There's no greater asset in America than being well known. I wouldn't call it Scandawools, it would be Nigel Newman and Co.—or just Nigel Newman, and we could possibly have retail outlets to cash in on your name. I might invest half a million in the set up, but your name alone's worth a million.'

'To the pastrami trade.'

'But it was a quality pastrami, wasn't it?'

'The best.'

'These are going to be quality garments, Nigel, I promise you we couldn't fail.'

'It would be too uneven. If I had a bit of money on my own—'

'I'd put in my money as a loan, to be repaid out of profits.'

'And how would you be repaid, out of losses?'

'Nigel, we'd be minting money.'

He thought for a long time, then he said: 'Dad, I think you've got yourself a partner.'

He had to leave the next morning for Las Vegas where he was due to appear in cabaret. He was in great spirits.

'It's a crummy show in a crummy joint,' he said, 'and, boy, do I look forward to telling them what to do with it all.'

The next few days were amongst the happiest in my life. I had Californian sunshine, plus life, plus hope. I had found Los Angeles vaguely attractive even in my dejected mood; it seemed paradise now. My mind was abuzz with ideas. It was as if I had never retired, but was merely re-deploying my assets. I felt a pang of regret that Dora was dead, for here, at last, was the sort of good news that I liked to bring home to her. I was not merely about to start a new life, but two new lives. I wrote to my Scandinavian suppliers to tell them of my plans and to a number of British manufacturers whose products I admired, asking them if they were represented on the West Coast.

I also began reading the trade magazines and wrote to my solicitor to discover exactly how much I was worth and how far it was possible to use sterling for investments outside the sterling area. I don't know what had made Dora think I wasn't much of a businessman. I was back in business and business was my life. I felt younger, fitter and even Mo was moved to remark: 'Zeida looks kinda different.'

I outlined my plans to Jo who threw herself round my neck before I could finish and she wondered, as I did, why I hadn't thought of it before. I had always dreamed of having Nigel with me in business, but always within a British context. The thought of settling in America had simply never occurred to me.

'We could lead a normal life,' said Jo. 'The kids would have a father, I would have a husband. The phone would no longer be an enemy.' She was ecstatic.

'Perhaps you'll be able to fit a joint product into your schedule,' I suggested.

'A joint what?' But I felt it was too soon to broach the subject.

'You know something?' said Jo, 'I'm glad his big break hasn't come. I was praying for it, but I was dreading it. If he'd made the big time we would hardly have seen him. Sure I'd have been happy for him, but I wouldn't be happy for us. You know what's good about God? He doesn't listen to our prayers, or only listens with half an ear.'

There was, however, one small cloud on my horizon and that was the recollection of Iris's visit. If she had managed to set up a Scandawools outlet in America then it was unlikely that we would be able to compete, but from what I could gather she hadn't got far. One needed people on the spot and that's exactly where we were. With my contacts and experience and Nigel's flair we could sweep America.

I wondered if it might be an idea to persuade Iris to join us. Our last meeting had left an unpleasant taste in my mouth, but that was probably because of Dora's unfortunate letter. Iris had always enjoyed working with me. There was, of course, less security to being part of a small organisation than a large one, but more fun. With her, Nigel and me, we could possibly re-create the golden days we had with Dave, though, of course, there could be no thought of her being a mere secretary (if there was such a thing nowadays). She would have to be a full partner. I put that down at the top of the agenda of things I wanted to discuss with Nigel as soon as he got back.

One evening Jo was at home to the local chapter of the Mamme Loshen League which, I took it, was some sort of Yiddish language society. I had always associated Yiddish with old age and poverty while here were prosperous young matrons playing at immigrants and talking about 'mine analyst' and 'heimishe crepe-suzettes' and 'low-calorie cholent' and 'polyunsaturated schmaltz'. I couldn't speak Yiddish but knew vaguely what it should sound like and it sounded wrong to me, but they obviously enjoyed themselves and so did I.

Jo had prepared what she called a heimishe buffet, consisting of a large variety of herrings on crackers, plus some very unheimishe dry martinis which, though served in the same measures as whisky were considerably more potent. Moreover, it was a hot day and they were deliciously thirst-quenching and after a few glasses I was on the verge of intoxication, which was a new experience for me and I found myself grasping arms and tapping knees with rather greater abandon than I should otherwise have done. No one actually protested, though to one attractive young woman who gave me what seemed like a disapproving glance after I had given her a playful pat on her thigh, I explained that I was 'a heimishe dirty old man'.

'Is there a Yiddish expression for that?' she asked.

'No,' said a stern voice behind me, 'in der heim, old men behaved themselves.' The voice belonged to what I gathered was the guru of the group, a plump, white-haired figure in thick glasses.

Apart from him and two Mexican waiters, I was the only male present.

One lady with white hair, blue eyes, leathery face and scarlet nails, who could have been thirty or forty or fifty, asked me what my name was and I said Sidney.

'I meant your Yiddish name.'

'Sidney.'

'What did they call you when you were Barmitzvah?'

'I didn't have a Barmitzvah.'

'No Barmitzvah?'

'But I was circumcised.'

'Everybody in America is circumcised,' she said disdainfully and walked off. I felt I had disgraced myself and possibly disgraced Jo.

One young woman had brought a guitar (in California they carry guitars much as they carry umbrellas in England) and towards the end of the evening she gave a recital of Yiddish songs, while the rest of the guests sat around on the floor. I couldn't imagine English women of that age (though it is difficult to age American women) and class, sitting around on the floor without looking slightly ridiculous, but here they not only looked right but rather exciting. Why did women look more alluring with their legs under them than sitting upright or standing up? They joined in the singing, swaying with the music. The melodies were familiar and melancholy, full of sad echoes. Some of the women were in tears. Who, I wondered, was looking after their homes? What had they done with their husbands and children? Did they all have ex-husbands who took their children out for the day?

When the last of the guests were gone, Jo said to me: 'You were very good and very helpful.'

'Was I? I thought I had disgraced you.'

'Oh, you mean because you told Ray you weren't circumcised?'

'I told her I was—though I suppose that isn't the sort of subject one should raise in polite company.'

'In California they don't raise anything else, but she hasn't had a man for years and you reminded her of what she was missing. You were quite a hit. "Is that your father-in-law?" they kept asking, "he's much better looking than your husband".'

'Everyone is better looking than your husband, my dear. Even his poor mother had to admit that his face wasn't his fortune, but the strange thing is he always attracted the most beautiful women—you for example." Her face glowed.

'Do you think I'm beautiful?'

'When you make the effort, as you did today. Strange that. Women never seem to dress up for their menfolk here, only for other women. I've been here over a month and this is the first time I've seen you in a dress.' It was a simple little frock of white, very thin muslin, almost cheesecloth, which brought out the firmness of her figure and her tanned limbs.

'Let's go for a drive,' she suggested.

'It's a bit late for an old Zeida to be out and about.'

'You're playing that old Zeida part for all you're worth, aren't you—it's to make women feel safe, but I think you're an old rake. I could see the way you were eyeing the girls—those weren't Zeidaish looks you were giving them.' She put her arms round my neck. 'You *are* an old rake, aren't you?'

'What do you want me to say?'

'I don't want you to say anything. I want you to put your arms round me.' I did as I was told. I liked her smell, a mixture of perfume, herrings and gin.

'Know something?'

'What?'

'You're afraid of me.'

'What's there to be afraid of?'

'Then why don't you hold me tighter?'

I held her tighter.

'That's better, that's nice.'

It was a warm night, heavy with the scent of flowers and dried grass.

'Want to come for a swim?' she said.

'At this time of the night?'

'It's the best time.'

'Who'll baby-sit?'

'I'll ask Laureen to come in for a minute. I've done the same for her, she'll understand. Come on. Let's.'

'I've already had a swim.'

'Have another.'

'My trunks are still drying.'

'Who needs trunks?'

'Who needs—I'm too old for that sort of thing.'

'You don't feel too old for anything.'

'Know something?'

'What?'

'I *am* afraid of you.'

'There's nothing to be afraid of, Zeida. Incest is ethnic. Think of Judah and Tamar.'

At that moment the phone went.

'Aren't you going to answer?' I said.

'There's nobody I want to hear from. Let it ring.'

'Shall I answer?'

She sighed and went inside. She returned a minute or two later looking mildly dumb-founded.

'Something wrong?'

'I'm not sure. That was London. He's got the part.'

# 6

When I got to Heathrow I wondered if I should phone
Gypsy. I wasn't particularly interested to talk to anyone or
see anyone and was anxious to get back to my own home, my
own bed and my own company and perhaps a bit of sea-
spray in my face, but if Gypsy had found out that I had
passed through London without phoning, she would never
have forgiven me. On the other hand she would start cross-
examining me in her lawyer's way, as to why I had left so
suddenly, why I had returned without notice, what I would
be doing with myself and I was in no mood for any of that,
but on an impulse I phoned her and a little to my relief one
of the maids came to the phone to say 'she a no in'.

'Could you give her a message?'

'A message?'

'Just say her father sends her love. He's back and he'll
phone her tomorrow.'

'He phone tomorrow?'

'Yes.'

'She a no in.'

'I know she a no in, but tell her her father phoned and
he'll call tomorrow.'

'She a no in tomorrow.'

And I left it at that. I had done my duty and dived into a
cab for Victoria.

It was odd to come into the house and not find Dora
there. That's when you feel a bereavement, when you return
to a familiar scene and come upon an unfamiliar gap.
David's office had been right next to mine. He was hardly
ever there, for he was on the road most of the week, yet for
months after his death I couldn't pass his door without a
pang. Nigel had snatched me off to America shortly after
Dora died and I didn't miss her in America because she had

154

never been part of my life there, but I became aware of her the minute I returned to Britain and the awareness grew stronger as I drew nearer to the coast and when I reached the house it was almost overwhelming. And we hadn't lived there for more than a matter of months. What would it have been like to return to Mill Hill?

But still it was good to be back home. I had been away for three months, which was longer than I had ever been away from England before and I missed it, the moist air, the temperate weather, the soft colours. I didn't know how people lived in California. It dazzled the senses and I suppose it was good as a pick-me-up. People kept talking about drugs and drug culture, but living in California was a drug in itself. I wanted to return to my usual self.

I turned on the gas, put on the kettle, got down the biscuit tin, switched on the radio. Now that was something I'd missed in America, the radio. There were a million stations, but they all sounded the same and all seemed to offer the same nauseating drivel and after a time I just switched off and stayed off.

The door bell rang. It was Telfer, standing a little hesitantly on the door step as if wondering if he should have called.

'Been away?' he said.

'Yes.'

'Thought you were. Place in darkness. Can't be away too long these days. Squatters, that sort of thing.'

I turned off the gas and poured a couple of whiskies.

'Your wife's dead, I hear.'

I nodded.

'Sorry to hear it.'

'That's life.'

'That's what?'

'Life.'

'Death you mean.'

'Where there's life there's death.'

'Is that what your religion says?'

'I'm not sure what my religion says—I'm not sure I have a religion.'

'You're—' he hesitated as if about to ask a very personal question, 'you're Jewish, aren't you?'

'Well yes, sort of.'

'You mean, like I'm Christian.'

'Exactly.'

'Difficult to know what you are once you stop going to church parades. That's the good thing about the army. Puts you in your place.'

We stared into our glasses for a time.

'She was the third woman in the street to go.'

'Who?'

'Old lady—bottom of the road. Took a long time going.'

'And who else?'

'The wife.'

'Whose?'

'Mine.'

'Kathleen?'

'Yes.'

'Dead?'

'Afraid so.'

'Had she been ill?'

'No. Picture of health.'

'That's how I remember her.'

'Never been ill in her life.'

'Then what happened?'

'Car crash.'

'When?'

'Last month. Total write-off. Car, I mean.'

'I'm sorry to hear that.'

'Wasn't my car. Embarrassing thing is she'd been carrying on. One wants to be broad-minded about these things, but at her age you'd expect her to behave. The chap survived, ex-wing commander. His wife nearly killed him though.'

I refilled his glass with a shaking hand and took another glass myself.

'Friend of family. Knew him from British Legion. Hadn't been coming lately, at least not much. Now I know why. Thought of joining? The British Legion, I mean.'

'No, not yet.'

'Your friend has. Small fellow. Home Guard.'

'Michaelson?'

'That's his name. Funny chap. Only comes on ladies' nights.'

'I might come along.'

'Do. Good company. Splendid club rooms. Marvellous bar. Bags of parking space.'

I sat down in an armchair after he left and must have fallen asleep for when I woke it was morning and it took me some time to recover my bearings. California, at that moment, seemed like a dream and the one thought that came to mind was my father's warning, 'Once you start sleeping after lunch, you're an old man.' But when did I have lunch, how long had I been here? Where was Dora? The last thing I clearly remembered doing was going into the supermarket with her and loading up the car with the week's shopping. Then we went into a coffee shop, did a bit of window shopping, took a look at the local library, then lunch. And after lunch, I suppose, I must have settled into the chair and fallen asleep. I was an old man. But where was Dora?

I went into the bedroom and then it all came back to me, like the flickering cards in one of those what-the-butler-saw machines, all in rapid succession. Ada. Kathleen. Shirley. Iris. Illness. The family assembly. Recovery. Relapse. Death. Funeral. Flight. California. Jo. Mo. Moishe. Nigel. And there the card stuck.

I felt like putting my head in a bucket of cold water to clear the confusion. Instead I had a hot bath. I don't know how long I stayed there, for the water was quite cold by the time I emerged, but it restored me to what senses I had left. I shaved, put on a tweed suit, went out to buy a *Daily Telegraph* and read it over breakfast in a local restaurant. I felt rather good, even elated. It was a sunny morning, but cool, with a brisk wind.

I then took a walk along the front and again felt that all that had happened in the intervening months couldn't have happened and when I got home Dora would be preparing lunch and we would eat together, I struggling to listen to the one o'clock news and she keeping up a commentary on the events of the morning. It was so unlike her to die.

I must have walked about a mile when I saw a familiar figure ahead of me, slight and slightly bent, but the most familiar thing was the walk. It was Michaelson, who, especially if in a hurry, moved with an odd whirling gait, as if he was riding a bicycle. I caught up with him and tapped him on the shoulders. He jumped and then peered at me closely.

'It's not Newman,' he said.

'Who the hell do you think it is?'

'I thought you had departed this life for California.'

'Well I've risen again.'

He grabbed my hand and took me to the cocktail bar of the Hotel Dreadful.

'It's an omen,' he said. 'The minute you tapped my shoulders I was thinking about you. I want to go back into business, but I need a partner.'

'What sort of business?'

'A brothel.'

'A—?'

'Brothel. The way you're looking at me you'd think you'd never been to one.'

'I have never been to one.'

'And you were five years in the army.'

'I was in the quartermaster's store.'

'What did you store?'

'Not what you think.'

'Well, I can tell you there isn't a place—at least not on the south coast—which you wouldn't be ashamed to be seen going into and even more ashamed coming out of. Sleazy

places which frighten the sex out of you and the sort of
women they have and the sort of surroundings and the sort
of clientele. Now, what I have in mind is a decent-looking
place, in a respectable location, well appointed, comfortable, even plush, where you could meet friends, read a
paper, have a drink, perhaps even a meal and then to round
off the evening with a—'

'You don't have to say it.'

'What's the matter, you getting squeamish in your old
age? The country, especially the south coast, is full of people
of your age and mine, with time on their hands and a bit of
money and more than a bit of lust—if only they could find a
decent venue. We could make a fortune, but it would cost a
good bit of money. I've done the arithmetic and you
wouldn't get much change from £200,000. Unfortunately
you can't go to the bank and say "I need a couple of hundred
thousand to set up a—." You don't look interested.'

'No, I'm just trying to work out if you're sane or not.'

'I've never been more sane in my life and we'd be per-
forming a public service. I could find a hundred thou if you
could.'

'I wouldn't if I could and in any case I see it as a way of
losing a hundred thou.'

'Losing money? You'd be minting it, you wouldn't know
what to do with it.'

'What would I do with so much money that I wouldn't
know what to do with?'

'Put it back into the business. We could start with one
place on the south coast, then open up in London and the
provinces, then Europe, after that, America. It's an area of
the leisure industry which the leisure industry's left
untouched. People live to all sorts of years these days. Their
stomachs become ulcered and shrivelled before they're fifty,
they're afraid of eating this because of their heart or their
stomach, they can't drink that because of their liver or
kidneys, they can't smoke because of their lungs, but what's
to stop them from having a bit behind the arras, as long, of

course, as they have the kit? It's the one healthy occupation left. It'll be a gold mine—remember the fellow who started the baby-goods business because of the baby boom, well the baby boom's spent, but you've got an old people boom instead. We could call the company Fathercare, or something like that. You should be able to think of a name— you're just back from America, they're good at names, the Americans.'

'The Dirty Old Men's Club.'

'You may have an idea there. Dirt's in, it's fashionable. Except that it's misleading. There's nothing dirty about a bit of fun. Why dirty? If a young man does it, people say, well that's doing what comes naturally, and if an old man does it, it's dirty. Why should the youngsters have all the fun? They've still got their youth and their energy. They should have better things to do with their physique. They can go skiing, sailing, climbing—'

'How much climbing did you do when you were a youngster?'

'When I was a youngster I had to earn a living, they don't nowadays. No, sex should be left to people of your age and mine who have nothing better to do with themselves and who can appreciate it.'

'Speak for yourself.'

'All right, I am speaking for myself—perhaps you're past it. It's the consolation for old age. Well, what do you say?'

'To what?'

'Are you coming in with me? You may be too old for sex, but you're not too old for money.'

'If I thought you were serious, I'd think you were mad.'

'Have you lost your business instincts?'

'I wouldn't mind starting up in a small way, a launderette or something.'

'A *launderette*?'

'Or ice cream.'

'Is that the limit of your ambition, an ice-da-crema parlour?'

'They've got very good ice cream in America, it's the best thing they've got. We could acquire a franchise here.'

'And sell penny pokes to snottery schoolchildren.'

'Better than selling five pound pokes to dirty old men.'

He came home with me for supper (I didn't have any tinned asparagus soup, so he brought some of his own), and I half thought of asking him to stay the night for I was a little uneasy about the thought of being by myself, but he had to go back to his wife, and when he left all the strange sense of well-being which had filled me for much of the day, petered out.

I suddenly felt sad, lonely, lost and even a little afraid. It was not late. I could get back to London and perhaps stay over with Gypsy.

When I tried to phone her, however, I got the same reply as the previous day.

'She a no in.'

'When is she coming back?'

'Not coming back.'

'When is she coming back?'

'She a no in.'

'Can I speak to Mr Nathan?'

'Mr Nathan a no in.'

'When is he coming back?'

'Mr Nathan?'

'When—' and I gave it up. In desperation I phoned Phyllis and Arthur answered, as I was afraid he would.

'Welcome back, globe-trotter! How is my famous brother-in-law and his infamous wife?'

'What do you mean, infamous?'

'All wives are infamous,' and he tittered at his own wit. 'Are we to be honoured with your company? Manchester isn't Hollywood, but what we lack in sunshine we make up for in rain. Hold it, my better half—in inverted commas—craves a word.'

'Hullo, Daddy, I never knew you were back.'

'I only got back yesterday.'

'We were all under the impression that you were stopping there for some time. I would love to see you. Can you come up?'

'Not immediately.'

'For the weekend?'

'The weekend. What day is it?'

'Tuesday. I don't like the idea of you being on your own and Gypsy isn't in town. I don't know where she is. I've tried her office, but they're cagey about it. I don't know what's happening.'

'When did you last speak to her?'

'Weeks ago and she was uncommunicative then.'

I put the phone down feeling deeply troubled, but slightly less vacuous. Worry was company of sorts.

I sat in the darkened room, gazing out at the street outside, towards Shirley's house, wondering if she had company. The house was in darkness. Perhaps she was in bed. Perhaps she was even dead. Everybody seemed to be dead, suddenly. It was the in thing. It was nine o'clock and not quite dark. I could see the reflection from Tefler's television set dancing on the grass outside and I could hear the sound of the nine o'clock news. I half thought of joining him. Instead I put on a coat and walked down towards the harbour to see if I could find Ada, but when I was in sight of her house, I hesitated and turned back. I couldn't do it to Dora. I couldn't quite make out how my mind — or was it perhaps my soul — worked, but I was being more loyal to her now that she was dead than I had been when she was alive.

When I got back Telfer was still by his television, presumably watching the ten o'clock news. There was not a soul in the street and no sound, except television announcers crackling like crickets.

I went back inside, sat down in an armchair without taking my coat off or putting on the lights, leant back and fell asleep. I was not so much tired as exhausted by sheer weariness of soul.

I phoned Gypsy first thing the next morning. It was still

'she a no in,' and I tried her office about an hour later and, as Phyllis said, her secretary sounded decidedly cagey: 'She'll be in later, but I'm afraid she's got appointments all day.'

'Could you ask her to phone me?'

'If I can get hold of her, Mr Newman, but I'm not sure if she'll have the time.'

Half an hour later the phone went. It was Gypsy. There was no sound of joy or greeting in her voice. She didn't even seem surprised I was back. There was also an unfamiliar gritty quality in her tone which troubled me.

'Jo phoned me yesterday. I was called out of a conference. She sounded very upset. She said she came back from work and found you in the middle of packing. Was she that dreadful?'

'Dreadful? Anything but—'

'She was too upset to go to work. She was at home in bed crying. What did you do to the poor girl?'

'Nothing. She was very good to me. She couldn't have done more to keep me happy.'

'Perhaps she did too much.'

'Look, we'll talk about Jo another time. I want to know what's been happening to you?'

'What makes you think anything's been happening to me?'

'Come on, out with it.'

'I can't speak to you now.'

'Shall I come up to London?'

'No, I'll come down. A night by the coast might do me good. Expect me about six.'

# 7

'Nathan and I are finished.'
'Divorced?'
'If only we were, but the bastard won't give me a divorce.'
I was shocked by her appearance even more than her announcement. She had lost weight (and she never had too much of it in the first place), her face was sunken, even shrunken and there were dark patches under her eyes which she tried to hide behind sun glasses. Worst of all, she had lost her perky, glittering quality. She looked haggard and something I never imagined she could be, drab.
'Will you stop staring at me,' she said impatiently, 'I know I'm no Botticelli.'
'Have you been ill?'
'I'm all right.'
'Do you want to have a rest or to lie down for a while?'
'Will you stop acting like a Yiddish mamma,' she shouted. 'I'm all right.'
'You needn't blow up in my face.'
'I'm sorry.'
After that I was a trifle hesitant about saying anything at all, but there was a lot I wanted to know.
'How did the trouble start?'
'With Nathan? From about the day we married, possibly before, but surely you must have known that our marriage wasn't much of a marriage.'
'Not many marriages are, but I was under the impression that you had worked out your own way of life and that you admired Nathan.'
'Oh, he's a great lawyer, an international figure, rich, handsome, a success, who doesn't admire that?'
'He's still successful and handsome and—'
'He's still everything, but it's not enough.'

164

'And it's taken you seven years to find that out?'

'It didn't take me seven weeks to find it out, but I thought I was expecting too much.'

'So what's happened to change things? Did you have some sort of jolt?'

'Didn't we all?'

'Your mother's death?'

'That was part of it.'

'There's something I don't understand, if you say your marriage has broken down, can he refuse to give you a divorce?'

'He can and he has.'

'Is that the law?'

'It's Nathan's law and if he doesn't want a divorce, I'm not in a position to demand one.'

'Are you trying to tell me he's blackmailing you?'

'Draw your own conclusions.'

'Nathan?'

'Yes, Nathan.'

'I'm sorry, I can't believe it.'

'I didn't think you would.'

'He's just not—'

She turned upon me with some heat.

'What do you know about him? What do you know about me for that matter? What do you know about any of your children? Do you know what's been happening to Nigel? Have you tried to find out? Nathan's a thug.'

She used to be like that as a child. It didn't take her long to calm down, which she did, with an apology.

'What has he got to blackmail you on?'

'Have you never done anything on which you could be blackmailed?'

'No, never.'

'Lucky you.' She hesitated. 'One of my clients was in difficulties, so I dipped my hand in the account of another.'

'One of your—! I should have a lawyer like that. But what made you do it?'

I'm not sure if it's any of your business.'

'None of this is any of my business, but don't you think I have a right to know?'

She was silent.

'How much was involved?'

'Forty thousand.'

'*Pounds*!'

'Pounds.'

'So what happened?'

'Nothing happened, Nathan paid up.'

'That was gallant of him.'

'Was it? What would it have looked like if the wife of the senior partner of Chisholm and Black had been struck off? So here I am, tied.'

'Why didn't you come to me for the money?'

'You?'

'I've got money, what do you think I'm saving it for, a rainy day?'

'Forty thousand pounds?'

'I could afford it.'

'Your hand shakes every time you sign a cheque.'

'Look, I don't throw it around, if that's what you mean, but in an emergency—'

'I wouldn't have asked you and you wouldn't have paid. You'd have told me to have my head examined—'

'I don't know what it's all about. Perhaps you should have your head examined.'

'See what I mean? And in any case you weren't here.'

'There's one thing I don't understand—there's many things I don't understand—but this in particular. Why should Nathan want to hold on to you if you're such an embarrassment?'

'I've often asked that myself. Partly, I suppose, because I'm a good lawyer and I've brought in some important clients. Partly because, I suppose, he likes me as an ornament at his dinner table.' She looked at herself in the mirror. 'I don't look much like an ornament now, do I?'

I didn't press her further. Instead we drove out for a meal and after a few whiskies and some wine, she looked better, or maybe she looked better because I had had a few whiskies and some wine. She became talkative and relaxed. I was anxious to know why she had needed that £40,000 so badly, but I was afraid that if I returned to the subject the congenial mood might change. Instead she kept pressing me about my stay in California.

'Aren't you going to tell me what happened with Jo?'

'There's nothing to tell.'

'Then why was she crying—'

'Well you know how it is with these tender young matrons—'

'Tender? She's as hard as flint.'

'You know her?'

'Of course I know her, I've met her a couple of times, once in New York, once in California.'

'Yes, I seem to remember her saying that, but you hadn't told me you'd met her.'

'She was a dirty little secret then.'

'You mean she wasn't married yet?'

'She was, but not to Nigel and they were living together. Nigel swore me to secrecy. He has sworn me to so many secrets that one day I'll burst with them. She's a very pretty thing, but omnivorous.'

'What do you mean?'

'She'll eat everything in sight. Did she have a nibble at you?'

'For God's sake!'

'Then why did you leave?'

'Can I change the subject?'

'No, you can't. I've always said if you must do something you shouldn't, the best place to do it is in the family. Everybody's got the same good reason for keeping it dark.'

She ate little and by the time we had finished the wine she was slightly tipsy and her words were becoming slurred. She asked for a brandy after the meal but I didn't think she should have one.

'It's my night-cap. I'll never get to sleep without a brandy.'

'I've got a brandy at home.'

'Is it Napoleon brandy?'

'It's a good brandy.'

'Want a Napoleon brandy—a large one.' She sounded a little like Moishe.

I sighed and called for the waiter.

She beamed at me mischievously through the huge bell glass as she drank it, as she used to when I bought her ice creams she didn't deserve. She hadn't changed all that much, a very pretty, very wayward child. And I was the same, indulgent, father.

She fell asleep in the car and I left her there while I went to the guest room and made up the bed and prepared a hot-water bottle. I then carried her in—she was as light as a feather—and began to undress her, taking off first her shoes, then her frock. Then as I was removing her tights she stirred and said sleepily:

'Daddy, remember I'm your daughter, not your daughter-in-law.'

I was up early the next morning to make her breakfast, but she was gone, with her bed neatly made. There was a note on the kitchen table with one word: THANKS.

I was anxious to speak to Nathan and a week passed before I could get hold of him, but the time didn't drag as it had done before. Anxiety and consternation and the many phone calls I had to make filled the days. At first I thought he was avoiding me, but in fact he had been abroad and had phoned me as soon as he got back and we arranged to meet for lunch the following day.

I came with a slight feeling of hostility, almost playing the role of the outraged father, but sat down opposite him with a pang of regret that I could no longer look upon him as one of the family. He had such a relaxed, gracious manner, I had felt that the family had been raised to a higher class through Gypsy's marriage. Now we were back among the plebs.

'Well,' he said, 'what shall we do about your daughter?'
I shrugged my shoulders helplessly.
'To be honest, I don't even know what it's all about.'
'You've spoken to her?'
'Yes, but the more she told me the more bewildered I became. Why did she need £40,000 so desperately that she had to embezzle a client's money?'

'It's all simple and I'm afraid, rather sad. She became infatuated with one of her clients, a young film-maker with a slight reputation and I would say even slighter prospects. He had some idea for a major film which he and she believed would establish him for life. Major films cost major sums. He needed half a million and she introduced him to various clients and friends, with some success, but he was still about £40,000 short, and when all else failed, she turned to embezzlement. I could see it happening, of course.'

'You did and you didn't try and stop her?'

'It was my one chance of stopping something worse than embezzlement. The money I could pay back and did. She's hoping to marry the young man, which would be a calamity beyond mending, for he is a squalid little creature — hardly more than a ponce — who lives off every woman he meets and I have no doubt that if he does marry her and she has outlived her usefulness, he will discard her as he has discarded all the others. I have taken pains to look into his history and I have a file on him as thick as a dictionary. But much as she is devoted to him, she remains devoted to her career — which gives me a modicum of leverage, for if she insists on a divorce I could have her struck off.'

'So that's what she means by blackmail.'

'I suppose one could call it that. She's a good lawyer, with a good brain, but for all her intellectual capacity, she is frightfully immature. I'm hoping, as no doubt you are, that she'll grow up, but I must admit that I occasionally despair.'

'How long has this been going on for?'

'It's been simmering for about a year, but only came to

the boil about the time your wife died. It hasn't quite come
off the boil yet.'

'How long can it continue?'

'Six months, perhaps a year.'

'As long as that?'

'What's a year to a lawyer? I'm not being vindictive, you
understand? If the young man was of sounder character
with better prospects, I would not have stood in her way.'

'Supposing this thing doesn't come off the boil?'

'It'll mean ruin, I'm afraid, irretrievable ruin, not only of
our marriage, but her life.'

# 8

We came to Crocus Hill in the winter and we had been
looking forward to the summer. 'We started in the worst
possible time,' Dora had said, 'rain, cold, wet, long hours
indoors.' We had planned to have friends down at weekends
once the better weather started and Phyllis had promised to
come down with the children (though without Arthur, who
had to go to America for some conference or other) as soon
as the schools broke up, but Dora went before the summer
came and I was wafted to America. And now I was back it
was almost autumn, or rather the sad end of summer, with
the days shorter, the beaches almost empty and the last
stragglers trying to snatch what there was left of sunshine
and warmth. I gazed at them and saw myself.

We used to take a house by the sea in Devon, Dora, the
children and I, the same house for four weeks every August,

with the children scampering among the sands like crabs. I
stayed one or at most two weeks and then joined the family
for weekends and we built sand-castles and flew kites and
played cricket and beach-ball and towards the end of the
day, when the tide was out and the sands glistened, we
poked around for shell fish in the rock-pools. Then Nigel at
thirteen decided to go to Scout camp instead of coming with
us and Gypsy at fourteen went to stay with friends and we
were left with Phyllis, dear Phyllis, who went everywhere
with us like an only child, until the day she married. She
met Arthur while on holiday. He was there with his mother,
tall and thin like himself, with big teeth (though without the
bushy moustache) and they looked like brother and sister,
except that they walked around arm in arm like lovers.

With the children married or away from home we started
taking holidays abroad, but didn't really enjoy them or at
least, never found them particularly restful. The sun was
usually too hot and the settings too exotic. They looked good
in a travel folder when read in January, but were a bit too
much when experienced in August. To me holidays always
meant sand and sea and the sight of children and the smell
of seaweed and the sound of seagulls and evening mists,
though the truth of the matter was that once the children
were grown up I ceased to care for holidays.

All our happiness, as Dora said, was built round our
children and all our efforts were on their behalf, but where
had it got us, or for that matter, where had it got them?
Phyllis, from whom we had expected least, had given us the
most satisfaction. But Nigel, what sort of life was he
leading, what sort of wife did he have, what sort of home?
Every time I thought back on those months in California, I
felt that they could not have happened and when it became
clear that they had, I shuddered. Nigel was solvent, which
was something, but what else had he achieved? What else
could he hope to achieve? My son the pastrami fresser. A
wasted, blighted life.

And as for Gypsy, I couldn't bear to think of her. I

staggered around in a daze for about a week after I spoke to
Nathan, until one evening Michaelson found me in a beach
shelter in the darkness, with tears streaming down my face.

'I honestly didn't think Dora meant all that much to you,'
he said. He came home with me and we made supper and
eventually bit by bit he got the whole sorry story out of me.

'You're crazy,' he said, 'you know that, don't you? Can't
you see you've built up some sort of fantasy and when
reality's fallen short of it you've gone to pieces. Gypsy's a
pretty child, lively, chutzpadik, bright, but she's nothing
out of this world and she's wilful, stubborn and spoilt. I
think you were carried away by the fact that a girl so pretty
who looked as if she was born for fun and play should not
only have got into university but should actually have qualified. I think people like you and me—but especially people
like you—who haven't been to university are a little over-
awed by those who have. When I was a young man nobody
thought of going to university unless he was specially
brilliant or felt an urgent calling to be a doctor or a lawyer
or a clergyman, or something like that. Nowadays any half-
baked idiot who can hold a book the right way up feels
entitled to a place at university and not only goes but is
actually paid to go. I employed a couple of graduates, if you
remember, relatives, otherwise I wouldn't have taken them
on as packers. Imbeciles, both. Trainee managers they were
supposed to be. They couldn't count, they couldn't spell,
they couldn't think, they couldn't manage. It was an
embarrassment to have them around when I had customers
in the place. I'm not saying Gypsy's like that, but believe
me, you don't have to be a genius to have letters after your
name or even to be a reasonably competent lawyer.'

'She's more than a reasonably competent lawyer—'

'In your eyes she is. Look, many fathers fall in love with
their daughters and especially Jewish fathers. I remember at
Gypsy's wedding—no, it wasn't the wedding, you'd got over
it by then. It was her engagement. You should have been the
happiest man in the world. Here she was about to marry

into the aristocracy, a nobleman, wealthy, handsome, distinguished, and a Jew—things which don't often go together, but you were sitting there with a drawn face and sunken chest as if your warehouse had caught fire and you'd forgotten to keep up the premiums. What's the matter with him I said, and Iris—a perceptive girl Iris—said to me, "He's just been thrown over by his daughter for another man." '

'You're fit company for my crazy American daughter-in-law,' I said. 'You've been reading too many psychology books.'

'Reading? I'm half blind, I can't read. I haven't opened a book in years.'

'Didn't you tell me yourself I was becoming a bore with the way I went on about my son-in-law? Gypsy's marriage was one of the great things in my life, can't you see? What's why I'm so upset.'

'It became one of the great things in your life, but that was later, when the years passed and she didn't have children and you began to think that perhaps she was only married in name and that she was still at least partly yours and that you hadn't lost a daughter, but had gained collateral, but now that she's got a boy-friend and the marriage has cracked up—'

'It's not only Gypsy,' I said.

'You can't have anything against Phyllis.'

'I've got nothing against Phyllis.'

'Ah, it's Nigel, the one who got away. Remember how we used to laugh at what your brother called the "Oi vay Hebrews" with the loud voices and the foreign accents and the gesticulating hands and we thought, or at least you and Dave thought, you were above them, that you were emancipated from their way of talking and living and thinking, but you're just the same. You don't mind your daughters doing their own thing—after a fashion—but you can't forgive your son for not being a prolongation of Sidney Newman and for not providing a grandson.'

'I can't forgive Nigel for having made a mess of his life.'
'Look, have you made such a success of yours?'

It had always been my good fortune that no matter how worrying things got I never had any difficulties in falling asleep. If I had any difficulties at all, it was in staying awake, but that night I couldn't get to sleep, nor the following night. I rolled from my bed to Dora's and from Dora's to mine. I got up, made myself a cup of tea and tried to read. I used to be a keen reader and had built up quite a library (mostly of paperbacks), but I was too weary to concentrate, yet not weary enough to fall asleep. I rummaged in Dora's bedside drawer and found a large assortment of pills, tablets, capsules. She used to take one of them to help her sleep, but I wasn't sure which. I felt tempted to swallow them all and in case I should, I rushed to the bathroom and flushed them down the toilet, or at least some of them, for the capsules floated stubbornly on top and I had to push them round the bend with a brush. I then got myself a very large whisky, put out the light and sat up in bed staring into the darkness till I could make out the various articles in the room, my valet-stand (a fiftieth birthday present from Phyllis), Dora's brushes and perfume bottles on the dresser. It was a sparsely furnished room, or rather all the furniture was built-in and one could, so to speak, pass a duster round the room without encountering an obstruction. Dora had been a little bit unhappy about the valet-stand which, of course, was not built-in and she was half inclined to throw it out, but I had had my way on that, for a change. I rarely had my way on anything else.

If Nigel had come into the business, as I had urged him to, I would never have sold out and Dora would never have pressed me to sell out. 'A tuppenny-halfpenny affair.' I was supporting fifty families on my tuppenny-halfpenny affair. I wondered how much he thought the sort of joys he had discovered for himself were worth. He'd been ready enough to join me when he thought he was finished, to use my experience, my contacts, my money. No more acting, singing, dancing, messing around, flying here, there and everywhere for the occasional cheque. He would settle down to a real life, doing a real job and perhaps start a family of his own. His play days were behind him. They were an extended fling, but behind him, or so he led me to believe, but one chirp from London and it was on with the motley. I didn't know who this Arky was who had arranged things for him, but if I'd had him within reach I'd have wrung his neck. He thought he was setting Nigel up for life, whereas he had killed his last hope—and mine. That had never occurred to Nigel, or if it did, it never bothered him. He came bounding back to L.A., thumping people on the chest, clapping their back: 'Well, what do ya think of the news, Dad, eh? Great, isn't it?' Didn't my face give him the answer and if it did, did he care? I even think he took a relish in my discomfiture.

'He likes to be independent,' his mother used to say and he refused anything I could do for him except money. He was costing me £1000 a year when he began in the theatre and £1000 in those days was money. I should have let him starve, it would have brought him to his senses. Of course I was spending more on Gypsy. Her flat alone cost me a fortune, but at least she was doing the right thing and if I was unhappy about her engagement to Nathan, it was only because he looked so much older than her and because he had been married before. He looked more like my generation than hers and he had the ridiculous habit of calling me 'Father' which made me feel ancient, but he soon gave that up, thank God, and I grew to like him and the irony of it now that he was no longer in the family I was more fond of him than I was of my own children.

Phyllis phoned the next evening to ask how I was and I said I was all right.

'You don't sound all right. Why don't you come up here?'

'To Manchester?'

'What's wrong with Manchester? Arthur's away and the

children would love to see you. They're all asking after you. Come up.'

'Perhaps I will.'

'I don't like the idea of you being there all by yourself. How are you coping?'

'I can make my own bed and fry my own egg. What's there to cope?'

'Have you nothing better to eat than an egg?'

'I have two eggs.'

'Dad, you're beginning to worry me. If you don't come up, I'll come down.'

With a threat like that, I promised to come up, but we didn't fix a date. With Arthur away she probably wanted my help to cope with the children. I had had enough of that in California to last me for life. And in any case where would she put me up? She hardly had enough room in her pokey little house for the children. When the youngest was born I offered them a couple of thousand to build an extension and Arthur was mortally offended. 'What sort of schnorrers do you think we are?' he demanded. But he was, on the other hand, prepared to accept a loan, and so a loan it was, though they hadn't paid it back, they weren't in a position to pay it back and I never for a moment thought that they would be. And in the end the money was used not for a bedroom, but a study, so that when we came up on a visit I slept in the lounge and Dora slept with the baby who wet his bed three times in one night and peed in her ear. Perhaps they were hoping for a further loan now. After all the old man's on his own and getting older. What does he need all his money for? When Nigel was in London he had borrowed my keys to come down and have a look at the house. I suppose he wanted to see if his inheritance was in good order. I had half a mind to leave it all to Nathan.

One of the bad things about sleeping badly is that not only do the nights seem endless but also the days, especially if you have nothing much to fill them in the first place. It rained almost continuously, so I couldn't have my usual walk. I tried Michaelson's house once or twice, but he seemed to be away. I sometimes watched cricket on television in the afternoon, but I would doze off then and wake up cold, shivering and wretched. A pity they didn't have all-night television, it might have got me to sleep.

I once, out of absent-mindedness rather than curiosity, wandered into the British Legion rooms near the station and I was greeted with a smell of gin and stale tobacco. Two elderly red-faced men were at the bar and another pair were in armchairs in a corner. Another much older man was assaulting a slot-machine with his stick and filling the air with curses. Heads swivelled round as I entered and swivelled back without a word of greeting and I was about to leave when a loud voice called out 'Ah, there you are,' and I found myself propelled towards the bar.

'Glad you could make it. Hoped you would. Splendid place, what? Let me introduce you to my friends.' It was Telfer.

'Piggy, meet my friend. Never did remember your name. Damned bad memory.'

'Newman.'

'Ah yes. Newman. Pay Corps?'

'Service Corps.'

'Whatever made me think of the Pay Corps? Yes, remember now. Service Corps. Of course, RTC.'

'QMS.'

'Of course, I should have remembered. Piggy here was APD in the RHA and George was VO in the AVC, or was it vice versa?'

George didn't answer or turn round.

'Stone deaf,' said Piggy in a whisper. 'Kicked by a stallion he was trying to castrate. Would have done the same meself. What's your poison?'

'A whisky, please.'

'Any particular type?'

'One whisky's as good as another to me.' Telfer coughed with what sounded like embarrassment.

'Try a malt,' he suggested.

'There's nothing like a malt,' said Piggy. 'Trouble is, once you've had a malt you can't touch the ordinary stuff. It's like sleeping with a black man—or so the wife tells me.'

The drink when it came almost filled the glass.

'A treble,' Piggy explained, 'life's too short for singles.'

'Can't have too much of a good thing,' said Telfer.

I liked the mellow taste of the whisky and its effect. I felt as if I was being infused with new and more potent blood and I finished the glass in a minute.

'Good show,' said Piggy, 'you people aren't too good at this sort of thing as a rule.'

'My people?' I said, 'what do you mean my people?'

'I didn't say *your* people, I said you people.'

'What do you mean by that?' And he exchanged a troubled glance with Telfer.

'Jews, I mean. Clever people and all that, but not very convivial. Chap comes here every Friday night, little feller, drinks Coca-Cola.'

'Michaelson,' I said.

'Home Guard.'

'Our MO was Jewish,' said Telfer. 'Splendid chap. Marvellous doctor. Never showed his face in the mess though. Said it made him giddy.'

Telfer stood the next round and I suppose I must have stood the third. I don't know what happened next, but whatever it was I slept well that night and for much of the following day, but the night after that I was again sleepless and I decided to see a doctor. Flecker himself was on holiday and I was treated by his locum, or maybe it was his assistant, a spotty youngster with furrowed brow and thick glasses.

'Do you normally sleep well?' he asked.

'Like a corpse.'

'Then why the insomnia? Is there something worrying you? Would you like to tell me about it?'

I looked at him—he could have been my grandson—and I decided I wouldn't like to tell him about it and he prescribed

some pills. 'Take one,' he said, 'two if you must.' To be on
the safe side I took three.

They worked all right. I don't know how long I slept till I
was awakened by someone rapping on my bedroom window.
My watch had stopped. I didn't know what time it was. I put
on my dressing-gown and staggered dazedly to the door. It
was Michaelson. He looked at me for a minute, then he said:
'Howard Hughes, I presume.'

'What's that?'

'Look at yourself. Half a beard on your chin, sunken
cheeks, matted hair and you stink to high heaven. I only
came back today and happened to bump into Telfer. "Have
you seen your friend?" he said, "looks a bit off colour."
When did you last have something to eat?'

'Before I went to bed, I think. Last night, I suppose.
What day is it?'

He took his coat off and began rummaging in the kitchen
cupboards.

'You've hardly anything in the house except digestive
biscuits and stale bread. Come on, get dressed, we're going
shopping. No, on second thoughts, I'll do the shopping and
you go and have a bath. And shave while you're at it.'

'What time is it?'

'Half-past five.'

'In the afternoon?'

'No, in the morning.'

'Everything'll be closed now, won't it?'

'There's always the Paki shop. Thank God for the Pakis.
It's good to know there's still people around willing to do
business. Why isn't your heating on by the way?'

'Heating? It's only September.'

'What's that got to do with it? It's cold. Get the heating on
and have a bath. I'll be back in a minute.'

I went into the bathroom and looked at myself in the
mirror. My face was covered with a heavy stubble, but I
didn't feel like shaving. It seemed silly to shave when the day
was nearly over. I was going nowhere. It didn't make much

sense having a bath or getting dressed either. But I ran the bath and had a wash all the same. I was drying myself when Michaelson returned.

'Why isn't the bloody heating on?' he roared.

I had forgotten all about it and in any case I didn't know how to fire the boiler, but there was an old electric radiator in the garage and we used that.

Michaelson had bought up half the shop by the look of things (including the entire stock of tinned asparagus soup) and he prepared an elaborate four-course meal.

'You know what I'm going to do when I get home tonight?' he said. 'I'm going to phone Gypsy.'

'What for?'

'You need looking after.'

'You want Gypsy to come here—'

'Or you to go there. You can't be left on your own.'

'What do you mean? I'm managing perfectly well.'

'That's what you think. If a sanitary inspector was to pass this place he would close it down as a menace to public health. You need somebody in with a shovel and spade to clean the place up a bit. Look at it. It's like a pigsty. Good God, if poor Dora could see it now, if she could see *you* now. This is you settling a posthumous account with a vengeance. You were fed up with her obsessive tidiness, now you're making up for it. What have you been doing since you came back, living on digestive biscuits?'

'Don't phone Gypsy,' I said.

'You can't expect Phyllis to come down.'

'I don't want anyone to come down. I'm all right.'

'You don't look all right.'

'I've been sleeping badly, but if I've got a medicine, I'll be all right.'

He couldn't stay long for it was nearly dark and he had to hurry back to his wife. He wanted to help me clear up, but I assured him I could manage myself. When I rose from the meal, however, I found that the slightest task, even moving the dishes from the table to the sink, required the greatest effort and after a few minutes I had to give up, exhausted. I sat in a chair and remained seated with my hands across my stomach, doing nothing, feeling nothing, or rather, a sense of conscious oblivion. Was I perhaps dead? Would someone come and lay me out and shut my eyelids and cover me with a shroud? And would a Rabbi then eulogise me as he had eulogised Dora? I had a reserved plot next to hers at Bushey cemetery. It was, as she said, a tidy cemetery. Willesden was no less tidy. That's where my parents were buried, with David alongside them. I had thought of reserving a plot next to David, but the cemetery was full. In any case what did it matter?

I don't know how long I sat there. I was vaguely aware of the rain falling outside and of the occasional passage of vehicles. I heard a car pull up and a door slamming shut and then hurried footsteps. The door bell rang. I felt too torpid to move. It rang again; I let it ring. There was silence for a while, then the sound of footsteps in the garden and the kitchen door opened and a tall figure entered in a suede coat and leather boots with the face half obscured by a plastic rain-hat. She removed the hat. It was Iris.

# 9

'I heard you needed company. So here I am, ever faithful, ever ready.'

She cleared up and washed up, talking over her shoulder Dora-fashion while she was doing it, though I wasn't quite taking it in, and I sat there watching her as if I was watching a kitchen-sink play on television, except that I managed to stay awake.

'How did you know I was back?' I asked.

'A little dickie-bird told me.'

'Michaelson.'

'It's years since I've seen him. How's his poor wife?'

'Same as ever.'

'Now there's a man who's had more than his share of adversity.'

'He's not the only one.'

She came over to me and waved a wet finger in my face.

'You, my man, are an ingrate. Wait till I'm finished, you're going to get a good talking to.'

She in fact took some time to finish, for she not only cleared up the kitchen, but took off her boots, tied a kerchief round her head and went on to clear the bathroom, remake the beds, hoover the carpets and do a Dora round the house, singing as she went. I had never known her to be so chirpy. It was all quite unnecessary, but I wasn't in the mood to argue about it. She then took me by the hand and led me into the bathroom and I was a little afraid as to what she might do next, but she sat me down in front of the sink, put a towel under my chin, got out my old cut-throat razor, stropped it with great deliberation and after waving it fiendishly round my head, began to shave me.

'You do it well,' I said.

'I know, I've missed my vocation. My old man was paralysed towards the end of his life, if you remember. I used to shave him every day.' When she finished she soaked a towel in boiling water and slapped it across my face. I nearly jumped out of my skin. She leaned over and put her cheek against mine.

'There, isn't that better?'

'Very much, I feel a new man.'

She then began to spruce herself up.

'Are you going back now?' I asked.

'No, I'm here for the weekend. Does that frighten you?'

'Is it the weekend already?'

'It's Thursday, but I feel entitled to a long weekend.'

It had stopped raining and she suggested we have a walk. We went out with me leaning rather heavily on her arm.

'Come on,' she said, 'for an old soldier you should be able to do better than that. Straighten yourself up.' I stood to attention. 'Now, by the right, quick march. One two, one two. At the double now. One two, one two, that's better.'

We were going down hill as Telfer, who was walking his dog, was coming up and he was startled by our approach, as was his dog. We kept up the pace all the way to the sea front and then took a long walk over the cliffs.

'Still upset about Gypsy?' she asked.

'Wouldn't you be?'

'I would never have built her up in my imagination in the first place.'

'No, it isn't that. What's upsetting me is that I can see a catastrophe building up in front of my own eyes and feel helpless to do anything about it.'

'If you ask me the catastrophe was her marriage.'

'You don't know Nathan. He's a noble man, I don't mean because he's from an old family and well connected, but he has noble ways.'

'Nobility's important to you, isn't it? You used to speak in the same way about Dave—'

'That was an older brother talking about an admired younger brother. Well, he did have a certain style—'

'A salesman's courtliness, except that he thought salesmanship was beneath him. And Gypsy, your insistence that she's a queen, was that a father talking about an admired younger daughter?'

'I suppose all daughters are queens in their father's eyes.'

'Phyllis wasn't.'

'No, perhaps not.'

'Actually Gypsy's boy-friend has a certain style.'

'Have you met him?'

'I saw him on television. He's quite well known.'

'Nathan mentioned his name. It meant nothing to me.'

'You don't mix in the higher—or is it lower—artistic circles. Very fetching young man.'

'Can you see them marrying?'

'Not for a moment, but I think she's working her way backwards towards normality. You see Gypsy, for all her gloss, is in many ways a typical little Jewish girl from a typical Jewish home, with the instinctive needs which go with that sort of upbringing. She always liked to think that she was above domesticity and family and children and regards herself as a thinking swinger, but thinkers don't swing and swingers don't think. Her marriage to Nathan enabled her to perpetuate the illusion, but it was unreal. You may think of him as blue-blooded, but I'm not sure if he had any blood at all. He doesn't strike me as quite human. She may spend a year or two with Shiran, but then she'll settle down with a nice Yiddisher boy, have nice Yiddisher children and be the comfort of your old age.'

I found the picture she was painting oddly discomforting.

I was a little apprehensive about the sleeping arrangement when we got home, but Iris made herself up a bed in the guest room. I got into my own bed and without the benefit of pills, fell asleep as soon as my head touched the pillow.

I woke before dawn feeling as clear-headed as I had felt befuddled the day before and with an odd sense of urgency, as if I had but a few hours to live and a whole world to put right. The first thing that occurred to me was that I had not yet made my will. I would drive into London immediately after breakfast and settle that with my solicitor. I wasn't too sure how much I was worth, but he would know. I knew exactly how I wanted to apportion it, but before that I wanted to have a word with Gypsy's young man.

I went into the bathroom and for the first time I realised how much weight I had lost in the past week or two. I was cadaverous, the prim little man Iris kept talking about, but, I'm afraid a prim little old man. My hair was much whiter—

bleached by the Californian sun—but the loss of weight
made me seem older and my nose much bigger. It had been
one feature among the others, but now it dominated my
face.

I phoned my solicitor at home. He was still in bed and was
startled to be called so early in the morning. He couldn't fit
me in at all during the day and suggested that I came the
following week.

'Impossible,' I said, 'it must be today.'

'Why the urgency? You're not likely to drop dead this
minute.'

'You can never tell.'

We finally arranged to meet for dinner in the evening.

Shiran proved rather more difficult to get hold of. I presumed Gypsy's secretary would have his address and tele-
phone number (he was, after all, a client) but she knew
nothing about him and Nathan's secretary was no more
helpful. Iris came into the room while I was on the phone
and I told her what I was trying to do.

'Is it wise?' she said.

'I don't know if it's wise, but it's necessary. I just want to
talk to him.'

'You're sure you don't want to horsewhip him?'

'I want to see what sort of creature he is.'

'A rather charming one from all accounts.'

'Have you got his number?'

'I could get it—but surely you're not going to see him
now?'

'Why not?'

'Are you up to it?'

'What do you mean?'

'Don't you know you've been ill?'

'Ill?'

'Very ill.'

'I don't know what I've been, but the fact is I feel all
right.'

'You don't look all right, and frankly you're not acting all

185

right. I'll be damned if I know what you want to see him about, but whatever it is—I'll tell you what, I'll go with you.'

'You'll do what?'

'I'll come with.'

'Look, Iris, I'm not married to you, and even if I was I'd resent your insistence. I'm not a baby. If you know the bloody number give it to me, if not I'll find it elsewhere.'

She looked at me in silence for a moment, then got me the number with the miffed air Dora used to adopt on the rare occasions she gave in to me against her better judgement. Strange how all women are alike—or was it only the sort of women I attracted?

When I phoned Sirhan, or whatever his name was, he sounded a trifle taken aback, even apprehensive, and he suggested that I meet him in a pub in the Fulham Road at seven o'clock. He said he was dark-haired, of middle height and would be wearing a blue denim suit.

'He's got a foreign accent,' I said.

'Didn't you know he was a wog?' said Iris.

Usually when I had to go into London, I dithered whether I should go by car or train. This time there was no dithering. I took my car and was delayed somewhat by a police car—a Jaguar actually—which gave me a ticket for speeding. Apparently a police Rover, which had tried to overtake me, had failed.

When I got to the pub the place was full of dark-haired young men in blue denim suits, but one of them detached himself from the crowd and came over to me.

'You must be Nigel's father,' he said.

'Nigel? How do you know Nigel?'

'What do you mean how do I know Nigel, he's going to be the star of my film.'

I had prepared myself for a confrontation with a villain. I wasn't quite sure what a villain looked like, for although I had known many foolish and vain men in my life, I don't think I had ever come across a downright wicked one, but here was a good-looking young man, perhaps a year or two younger than Gypsy, with plump, dimpled cheeks, smiling light-brown eyes, good teeth and a blue chin, but I didn't like the way he looked at me with a mixture of amusement and contempt.

'She didn't tell me anything about Nigel.'

'I should imagine there's a lot she didn't tell you, but does she have to? She's a big girl.'

'She's a married girl.'

He gave a laugh, as if to say, and what the hell has that to do with it. It was, I suppose, a fastidious point to put to a contemporary young man.

'Did she tell you she's been trying to get a divorce?'

I nodded.

'And did she tell you why she couldn't get one?'

'She didn't, but her husband did.'

The look of amusement went out of his eyes.

'She didn't tell you how it all began?'

'No.'

'She's my solicitor and I asked her to help organise a loan—'

'When I want a loan I go to my bank manager.'

'I went to my bank manager, I went to several, but I couldn't raise the sort of money I needed and I asked if she could help. She has wide contacts and she was very helpful. I did *not* ask her to put her hand into anybody's pocket, not even her own. I intended the whole thing to be a straight-forward business investment. Nathan knew what she was doing all along but didn't interfere till he could pounce—'

'He paid back the money.'

'He'll get it back, every fucking penny, with interest, but what's £40,000 to him? He's not interested in the money, but it's given him the screws on her.'

'I think he's doing what's best for her.'

'Do you? I don't, she doesn't and if you'll get to know your son-in-law a little better you may discover that he doesn't do anything unless it's good for Nathan. Why do you think he's holding on to her? Because she's his only true love? I'll tell

you why. She's a valuable property. All those Arabs lining
his office, who do you think brought them in? She did. She's
not only a partner, she's bait. What she lent me was
peanuts.'

'£40,000, peanuts?'

'£40,000? It was £100,000.'

'She said £40,000.'

'She used £60,000 of her own and borrowed £40,000.'

'Which makes it worse.'

'I had raised nearly £400,000 myself. The idea was that I
should raise half a million and my partner half. He'd raised
his part and because I was £40,000 short the whole deal
threatened to collapse. She wasn't slipping me a wad under
the table, you know. Your daughter's no dumb brunette, it
was a proper business contract.'

'When did Nigel come into it?'

'When he was here in the winter. She brought him in.
He's OK but no better than a hundred others.'

'And when it's all over, what?'

'She'll get all the money back—in duplicate.'

'I'm not talking about the bloody money. What'll happen
to Gypsy—her marriage?'

'Her marriage has already unhappened. She's living with
me, didn't you know?'

I wandered round the streets in a slight daze, partly
because I couldn't put my thoughts in order and partly
because I couldn't remember where I had parked my car. It
was a wet, cold, blustery night and the feel of the rain on my
face cleared my head a little; it was like sea-spray. I found
the car eventually and sat in the front seat gazing out
vacantly at the falling rain and the glistening street. Then,
as I was inserting my key into the ignition I saw the young
man coming up the street on the opposite side of the road,
hunched against the rain. There in that slightly pudgy little
figure was embodied the source of all my misfortunes. But
for him Gypsy would never have left Nathan. But for him I
could have set up in business with Nigel. But for him I

could have embarked upon a new life with new prospects. But for him . . .

I could not even remember starting my car, but then, when he was about twenty yards ahead of me I suddenly accelerated and shot across the road like a rocket. It couldn't have taken a second before I hit him and even within that time I heard a voice shrieking in my head — for Christ's sake, what are you doing?

I braked violently but too late. There was a loud bang and flying glass, the smell of burning rubber and hot metal and the feel of blood in thick, warm splotches. 'I hope it's mine', I kept thinking as I passed out.

# 10

Dearest Mo,

It was kind of you to write and to send me the parcel of pizzas, though I don't know what's made you think I'm hooked on pizzas, for I'd never tasted them before I came to America and I won't be sorry if I shouldn't taste them again. Still I appreciate your gesture.

You must be very clever to be doing a project on the criminally insane and I'll help you as best I can, but should warn you that my memory is not what it was, so don't rely absolutely on everything I tell you.

First of all, did I kill him? Well my lawyer tried to argue that the road was wet, that the hour was late and I was tired, that the car skidded and that the whole thing was an accident, so I stood up to say that my car had new tyres, it didn't skid, I knew what I was doing and that I was driving at the chap with the express intention of running him down, whereupon the lawyer entered a plea of diminished responsibility, which is why I'm here, in what you call a 'booby hatch', I call a lunatic asylum and they call a mental hospital.

As for the physical details 'whether his guts were splattered' all over the ground, I can't tell you a thing. Something was splattered, but whether they were his guts or mine, I'm not sure, though if they were my guts they must be something you can do without, for I'm feeling fine. I'm eating well, sleeping well and have put on weight. I've also recovered my reading habit, which I almost lost after I married (if you had met my late wife, you'd have understood why). They have a good library and reading rooms and a writing room and the whole place is like one of those huge Victorian hotels which has come upon hard times, which is to say, the service is not what it was. It's not enough to throw a fit to catch the attention of a nurse; what you have to do is to grab hold of someone by the throat.

The doctors are all either young men at the beginning of their careers or old ones at the end of them. My own doctor is a young man, a manic-depressive and he says our sessions together cheer him up no end. He's also trying to encourage me to keep a diary, which I'm too lazy to do, but instead I write letters to almost everybody I know and he makes copies, so anything you see here has been seen by other eyes and, for all I know, censored (which reminds me that your pizza looked as if it had been knocked about a bit, in case, I suppose, you'd used it to smuggle in a file, or something).

Now what else do you ask? 'Was his face blue?' I can't say, it was a dark night and for the same reason I can't tell you 'whether his tongue was swollen or not', but as he was dead when they found him, he couldn't have been a pretty sight.

As for the car, I don't know what happened to it. The radiator, which was dented, was an exhibit at the trial, but I don't know what they did with the rest of the car. I think it was claimed by my son-in-law, in which case what happened to my victim should happen to him.

Your last question: 'What do you do to satisfy your sexual needs?' puzzled me a bit, as I'm not sure that I have sexual needs and if I have, they're not crying out for satisfaction and I'm not on sufficiently intimate terms with the others to ask them what they do. It may even be that they do without.

I'm not sure what 'frontal lobotomy' is so I don't know if they go in for it. I don't know what proportion of the prisoners (or patients, as we are encouraged to think of ourselves) are sexual offenders and I don't think they castrate any of them, at least not by way of punishment. My doctor said that we're not here as punishment but as a cure, which makes it all sound a bit like a health farm, and I asked him what does one have to do these days to be punished, which left him stumped . . .


Dear Jo,

Thank you for your letter and your parcel and the photographs of the children; they're a pleasure to look at. Thank you also for Moishe's collage which you call breakfast time. How did he get together something so beautiful just with bottle-tops, cereals and honey? He's quite an artist and to judge from the sort of letters I get from Mo she should soon be a university professor, though I hope her interest in murder is only academic.

I shall enjoy the crystalised fruits you sent me, but they look after us very well and serve us more food than I can eat. They've also got spacious grounds and I can have long walks, but I miss the sea. A pity they don't have lunatic asylums by the sea except, I suppose, half the inmates would jump in if they did. As it is, every now and again somebody hangs himself, but they do that outside as well. Last week my doctor hanged himself. A nice young man, everybody liked him, but a bit neurotic. He said I was ceasing to respond, which left me feeling a bit sulky and since then I've been responding for all I'm worth.

The company varies. There's chaps here shuffling round, with long empty faces, not saying a word and looking how I felt when I first retired. Others keep laughing or clapping their hands and some can't stop talking. The first thing they ask you is 'What are you in for?' Like the 'Do-you-come-here-often' gambit in the dance halls and more often than not it's for wife-slaughter. In fact, killing your wife seems to be so commonplace a thing that you begin to wonder why they put people away for it in the first place. Here and there you find a mild, little, washed-out man, who'll tell you he killed his father, which sounds like a really wicked thing to do, but that's maybe because I'm a father and not a wife, but most of the people don't say anything at all, or mumble or never finish their sentences. They've been in for years many of them with nothing much to do and I suppose if they're not mad by the time they come in, they're mad by the time they get out. Some have forgotten what they're in for and are no longer interested in getting out. One of the chaps, a solicitor, who ran amok and killed a client, said that what keeps you going for the first month or so is the hope that you might be able to hang yourself. He was a POW during the war and it was the same thing there, he said, only, of course, they tried to escape then. Here hanging yourself is a way of escaping, but it's not easy because they watch you day and night. He did try to hang himself from his shirt once, but he's a stout man and it couldn't take the weight. It wouldn't have happened to a Turnbull and Asser shirt, he said, but this was a Marks and Spencer job. It's when you give up trying to hang yourself that you give up hope, he said (I don't know why I'm telling you all this. I suppose it's because I think Americans understand lunatics, they being half-way there themselves).

We have a Rabbi here, a meek little man, small, white face in a great black beard. He had a parishioner coming to him all the time asking if her chickens were kosher. She must have eaten a chicken a day because she was at his door every day. Finally it was too much. He grabbed the bird and set about her, which is not the sort of thing a Rabbi's supposed to do and he's been here for some time. Happiest man in the place, studying all the time. He's got lots of visitors, nearly all bearded and he keeps telling them if they want peace of mind they should do what he's done and set about their parishioners. It doesn't have to be with a chicken, he said, a goose or a leg of mutton will do (though I suppose a ham wouldn't).

My daughter Phyllis comes to see me quite often all the way from Manchester, though in fact I'm not quite sure where we are. There's so many Irishmen about so we could be in Ireland. Half the doctors are Irish (you can tell the doctors apart from the rest because they wear white coats) and the other half are Jewish, more than half maybe and I get the feeling that madness is a Jewish speciality—like the fur trade.

Gypsy doesn't come to see me at all, or write. I suppose she's a bit cross with me for doing what I have done—I would be myself in her place, but I thought she might have got over that by now. That's what I miss most, her and the sound and sight of the sea. I asked Phyllis if she sees anything of her, but she's not an easy person to talk to, Phyllis. She comes in tears and goes in tears and in fact I'd rather she stopped in Manchester. Perhaps they stop Gypsy from coming as part of the punishment, or maybe as part of the cure, only I'm not sure what I'm supposed to be cured of . . .


Dear Dora,

I suppose you must think I'm mad writing to somebody who's been dead all this time, but when you're in a mad house, doing something mad seems the most natural thing to do. You act up to what's expected of you. In any case I write letters to all sorts of people, which I never send off, which is a pity, for they don't charge you for the postage and I don't often get the chance of getting something for nothing.

I used to write to Gypsy every day, sometimes twice a day, but she doesn't answer. I only hope she's all right. I suppose she is, because they let you out for funerals, unless you're violent, which I'm not (unless killing that chap was an act of violence, which maybe it was, but I don't think I would have done it had I been on foot). Cars make killers of us all. I wished I hadn't done it even before I did it, but even as I was wishing, it was done. Terrible thing, cars, I suppose that's why you were always afraid of my driving. I don't feel too bad, or at least if I do, I take one look at some of the others and feel better. Here I am, seventy, or eighty is it (it's not that you lose all sense of time, but time stops being important and in any case they've taken away my watch — I suppose in case I might hang myself on the watch-strap)? Anyway, here I am, a man of advanced years and never been in an asylum before. I sometimes wonder how I got away with it.

It's a bit like the army here. Regular hours, regular meals, church parades, medicals, only no kit inspection and you don't know when the war'll be over (you didn't in the army either), or whose side you're on (you sometimes had doubts, even in the army).

They're a bit of a let-down, asylums. No chaps with funny hats thinking they're Napoleon or anything like that, though there's any number grinning to themselves or talking to themselves, but you have them outside as well (or you did — things may have changed since I was in Civvy Street).

It can get tiring doing nothing when you've nothing to do. This is retirement with a vengeance, but still I mustn't grumble. It took them nearly seventy years before they caught up with me and I've had all those years on the outside. Perhaps I was entitled to have them, perhaps not and when you start grinding people up under your car wheels you do become something of a nuisance. I'm not complaining. I did the wrong thing, running him down and they did the right thing running me in, but a chap does begin to have doubts about his own sanity once you lock him up in a lunatic asylum.

I see a good bit of Phyllis. How old is she now? She's getting heavy and tired-looking and in fact looks more and more like you, poor thing. Arthur's a full professor now, you know. She keeps apologising that he doesn't come and keeps threatening to bring him. I don't know what I'd do if he did come. You get to feel that you could do almost anything you liked and get away with it, because once they've put you away, they've put you away.

I had a bit of money, but I'm not sure what's happened to it—about £300,000 in fact, is that a lot these days? I think Nathan's looking after things, but I don't hear from him, or at least I haven't done since I've been inside, though perhaps he's abroad. One good thing about having a rich man looking after your money is he's less likely to steal it. Arthur's nabbed my Alvis. If he drives it like he drives his Austin, we shouldn't see much more of him (or the Alvis), but still, I don't like the idea of having such a lovely car in such clumsy hands. I was thinking of leaving it to Gypsy, but I don't see anything of her or hear anything about her. I don't see anything of Nathan, either, but I suppose he's abroad. Maybe she's abroad too. Isn't this the time of the year they go to Jamaica?

Iris is here almost every day. I keep asking her who's looking after the shop and she says a well-run shop looks after itself. She's seeing doctors and lawyers and even Members of Parliament (what have they to do with it?) and says she'll have me out in a week or two. She says that accident was an accident and I said it wasn't and that I went for the fellow and she said I must have had a brain-storm. Perhaps I did, but people who have brain-storms should be locked up. I asked her what I would do if they let me out and she said I'll find things for you to do, in that purposeful way of hers which makes me think that I'm perhaps better off where I am.

I've seen a bit of old Leslie. He was all right until a month or two ago, but fell out of bed, which you might think is a minor matter, except it was a bunk bed with the bottom bunk let to a lodger even older than himself. He's been a bit poorly since but he comes at least once a week, leaning on two sticks and we sit together talking about old times, when everything was about a penny a pound or a penny a pint or tuppence a ton or three ha'pence a yard. He also came to one of our Sunday evening evenings and did impersonations of Stanley Baldwin and Lloyd George and told jokes, until one of the patients tried to impale him with a broom handle and he hasn't been back.

I also get visits from an elderly man in black, some sort of chaplain I suppose, who keeps talking to me about God (though come to think of it, he may be an inmate — the man in black, I mean, not God). I think people take it for granted that once you're round the bend you must be religious (or maybe once you're religious, you must be round the bend).

There's all sorts of chaps keep latching on to you and the worst thing about being locked up, I suppose, is that you can't easily get away from people you'd rather get away from. The other is that people you'd like to see, you can't. You miss familiar faces, though if you look hard enough for them you begin to see them if they're there or not. I've seen the face of poor Dave on more than a dozen people and rushed towards them shouting 'Dave, it's me, Sidney' and they look at me as if I was mad. I'm beginning to see Gypsy's face too. I'd have seen yours, if I looked for it hard enough. Or a familiar street. If they only took us out once a week — in a caged lorry if they want — just to have a look at say Mill Hill or the sea. I miss the sea.

The funniest thing happened yesterday. I was walking in the garden when I felt a tap on my shoulders. I turned round and there stood a withered little man with pointed ears just like Michaelson.

'Mr Newman, I presume,' he said.

'It isn't Michaelson?' I said.

'I wish it wasn't,' he said, 'but I'm sorry to say it is.'

'Are you visiting?' I said.

'Visiting?' he said, 'you don't read the papers? I did in what's her name.'

'Your wife?' I said.

'Yes,' he said, 'should have done it years ago. There was a bit of a to-do about it. Trials, re-trials, medicals. Nearly drove me mad. Her family was anxious to show she died in her sleep—as if it was a reflection on her good character to say she was murdered. Anyway, it's why I couldn't come to visit.'

'What made you do it?' I said.

'Your example,' he said. 'I said to myself, if Newman can kill a complete stranger, why shouldn't I kill my own wife?' And he pulled me aside. 'Not too bad in here is it?' he said, 'Have you seen the nurses?'

'The nurses?' I said.

'Yes,' he said.

'I don't think you'll get a quick bit behind the arras round here,' I said.

All that, as I said, was yesterday and although I've searched high and low, I haven't caught a glimpse of him today. Could I have imagined it? I thought I saw him and he thought he saw me, but maybe we were both mistaken . . .